Erotic & Romantic Poetry

II

Published by Vantage Point Publishing
Indianapolis, IN 46229

ISBN 978-0-9883939-7-4

The publisher would appreciate notification where errors occur so that they may be corrected in subsequent printing and/or editions. Please send comments to the publisher by emailing to biz@amorousink.com

Printed in the United States of America

Dedication

Special thanks to all the featured artists who made
this book possible, Carl Patrick Dunford, Adriana
Smith, Dawn Rivers, and Flenardo Taylor.
And I would also like to thank all my readers and
Facebook friends specially, Barbara Wangari, David
Muigai, Jennifer Womack and Jennifer Weiffenbach ,
whose immense support has been the ink that fuels
my pen and resolve to achieve new heights each a
new day.

Cover Art by Darryl Blanchard.

Introduction

Enjoy the ride as the 4 poets with diverse talents take you for a flight laced with romance mastery and delicate eroticism that will waft your senses like burning incense in the alter of passion, provoking your whoremones, wetting your mind while satiating your appetite to the letter.

Definitely not to be rushed through like a college kids procrastinated homework but rather sat with for a while Savoring it like your favorite cocktail.
Not something to swirl and swallow like rum shots but rather to be sat with for a while seething with your tongue, teasing out the subtle flavors from every poem, every verse and every line to its sweetest end.

Satisfucktion guaranteed.

TABLE OF CONTENTS

Lyrical Poet

Real name, Patrick Kokello.
But popularly known by his pen/stage name Lyrical Poet.
He is the Author of **Hip-Hope Poetry** and **Erotic & Romantic Poetry Vol. 1,** also featuring 3 other poets.
By profession he is an environmental health & safety advisor in Canada's Fort McMurray oil sands.
By passion, he is a Poet/Author with a penchant for erotic & romance writings.
Originally he is from Kenya but currently living in Canada.
He started writing in 2007 while attending college in the USA, after his emotional poem "I remember being loved" won the Bainbridge College Coffee House literary contest.

His favorite line is
"50% I don't do what I write and 50% I don't write what I do".
Check out for his upcoming steamy erotic novel **Vacation/Fuckation.**
When does your vacation turn into a fuckation?.

Lyrical poet can be reached at,

Lyricalpoet@live.com.
 Www.Facebook.com/lyricalerotic

1) One wish

If I had one wish

I could wish to be a scarf

A light blue winter scarf

Of your favorite hue and dearest treasure

Wrapped around your neck

Keeping u warm and cosy

All night long

If I had one wish

I could wish you were the jasmine flower

Towering on my bedroom window

That I may wake up to ya alluring feminine scent

And the ambience of ya flawless beauty

If I had one wish

I could wish to be the evening breeze

Gently swishing through the cracks

Whispering the music of your splendor

Teasing your face yet fanning ya brow

Appreciating the beautiful you

If had one wish

I could wish to be joyfully invisible

That I may touch and feel you freely

That I may deeply stare into ya sexy eyes

And drown in their splendid gaze

With a desire to hold u without guilty

To love and cherish you without remorse

To embrace you with a favor that needs no control

And lastly

If I had one wish

I could wish that your skin was the canvas of my artistry

And my tongue was the paint brush of yonder

Drooling infinite love notes on your body

From the indention of your neck to the back of ya knees

Making your toes curl and coil with ecstasy

2). Have you seen her?

Have you seen her?

That woman

The lady in the streets but a freak in bed

Who loves to play with pots and pans

But can also conjure plots and plans

In the morning she is striking a business deal

In the evening she is fixing a delicious meal

At night my clothes are hers to peel

From dusk to dawn her heat to feel

Have you seen her?

That woman

Who says she independent but

Still needs a man

Not really for his money but honey in bed

The man who kisses her from her forehead to her toes

Provoking her whore moans making her cream

Taunting her demons making her scream

Awakening her neighbors from nirvana dreams

Have you seen her?

That woman

The one who will make me her Christopher Columbus

To explore her body like the vast America

Hiking her mountains at a pleasurable pace

Traversing all contours with a gentle caress

Discovering all her zones beyond the bend

All the erogenous zones in the deepest end

That no boy or BOB (battery operated boyfriend) can reach to scratch.

Scratch to relieve that sexual itch

Have you seen her?

That woman

The boardroom mistress

But bedroom whoretress

Who will torment my senses

With her constant teases

Assault my body with chains n whips

Fuck me mentally with her freakish talk

Let her blindfold me with her sensual thong

Kick her heels and get on top

Ride my tool like it's her full time job

Wringing me dry like a piece of cloth

Have you seen her?

That woman

The one that I long to meet

To her I surrender my sexual inhibitions

From her to gain my sexual liberation

Have you seen her?

That woman

If you see her

Please give me a call

1800 lyrical poet

3) I remember being loved

It was January I remember

I remember when I met her

In that telephone booth

When I gave her words

Her heart to sooth

In her I saw the ember

To light my hearts chamber

It was January

I remember

I remember in March

When I stopped the search

After talking much

About our likes and such

We made a perfect match

Our love was hatch

Our role was to thatch

It was March I remember

I remember in May

I remember that day

I remember it like yesterday

When I wrote her a poem

My feelings to essay

My love to display

I remember it was May

By my side she lay

Burbling from foreplay

I remember

I remember in June

How her name was my iTune

I wrote it on walls

On stalls in the malls

Inscribed it on rocks

And deep down in my heart

How I adored her

No me without her

Our love looked immune

From haters to prune

It was June

I remember

I remember in July

I remember truly

How we were all over each other

Like birds of a feather

Flying together

Aiming higher

To the sky and further

The storms to weather

I remember it was July

I remember duly

I remember in August

I remember how just

It wasn't about the thrust

Nor the lust

But the unquestionable trust

No need to spy

No asking why

All was in bliss

From hugging to the kiss

I remember August

I remember how just

I was madly in love

With my angel from above

I remember

I remember September

Just like October

How she made me sober

When she called me from slumber

With a hidden number

I remember her words

Piercing like swords

When she closed the curtain

Leaving me in the rain

With unbearable pain

I remember

I remember November

Just like December

How I hoped to outgrow

The wailing in sorrow

Like there's no tomorrow

I remember.......

How she became an issue

No longer to pursue

But sue with a tissue...

I remember with disgust

When I remember how fast

I became her past

When I thought it could last

Beyond August

I remember

Had to ponder

I can only wonder

What was the blunder

That made us asunder

After one year on the calendar.

I remember in tears

When I remember

My x

4) trEAT your woman right or another man will

I thought of you today

Of the sweet moments

we shared

Of your lovely ways that portrayed how much u cared

N I feel like a loser because I never reciprocated.

I thought of you today

Of being woken up to an orgasmic head

That was always accompanied with breakfast in bed

Sorry gal that I never treated u as befitted

N I hate imagining that another man has taken the lead.

I thought of u today

Of your sweet kisses and warm embraces

Never thought

 I'd wake up to your packed suitcases

Never thought

u'd leave without any traces

Never thought

That another man would be taking u places

I thought of you today

N I regret that I took you for granted

N I regret sitting here counting my loses

But I guess that's life's many faces.

Sometimes it deals u with the roughest of aces

A wake up call to the adage

"TReat your woman right or another man will''

5) Just a simple fuck

He stole her heart from heavens gates

With flowers and Chocolates in lavish dates

In him she saw the perfect mate

The prince charming knight to bind her fate

Playa playa he had his eyes cast on the prize

And to it he was willing to pay any prize

Days proceeded by, her heart was mellowing

But so were her thighs in accordance to his play book

Two weeks later he had her on his blood stained bed

Lavishing her virginity with wild abandon

In her heart she knew he was to be his first and last

But untold to him she was just simple lust

It's sad that when a gal thinks that sex is zeal

But on the other hand the guy knows that after sex it's a done deal

Sad that she bestowed her trust and feelings in him

Unknowingly that to him

She was just a simple phuck

6) I miss...

I miss the moments and comments we shared

When our fingers wriggled and I told u I cared

When we brushed shoulders and tangled legs

By the sprouting flowers behind the balcony

I miss your scent and ambience of the sunset

As the orange rays disappeared into the horizon

I miss the creases I imposed on your garments

As we rolled in the grass caressing freely

Our eyes interlocked midair with lust

Sourcing intervention from the Greek gods of love

I miss your hands exploring my pockets

Causing chaos within my briefs

I miss the caress of your Midas touch

Fishing it teasing it making me squirm

Weakening my senses for your goddess body

Yet strengthening the embers of desire for you

I miss undoing the snaps of your bra

Revealing those Pamela Anderson's pointed at noon

I miss traversing your mountains and contours

To the moist edges and hedges of the forest

As I drew you closer showering you with kisses

To the cheering of crickets and whistling thorns

I miss the pain of your nails on my back

Burrowing tattoos of your lust on my skin

As our hips and lips collided in ecstasy

To the thunderous moans and groans of splendor

I miss the trickling beads of sweat

From the siege & rage of virgin emotions

As we toiled and moiled to our first touch

Remember we were young and u said "not there"

Unlike nowadays I hate when you ask "honey are you there?".

The path was unfamiliar to my innocent spear

No wander the pain that you had to bear

I miss the sight of your chlorophyll stained hair

I miss the sight of green grass painted red

As we bade bye to virginity to love discovered.

7) A woman's 3 Fs

If u don't feed-

her

u don't fuck-

her

u don't finance-

her

Then shut the fuck

up!

If u aint know the color of a thong

If aint know the source her make up

If u aint know when she happy or not

Then u don't fuck her

U don't finance her

U don't fuck her

So shut the fuck up!

U tag urself in her pics

U have them in ur phone as ur screen saver

U gang ur boys for a slideshow

U tell them she urs she is a no go zone

But in reality she doesn't know u

U just a secret admirer

Showboating to up ur pride

That u fuck her on a regular (in ur dreams)

For if u did u could have known her favorite position

U could have known her favorite food

U could have known her favourite designer wear

So if u ain't feeding…her

U ain't fucking…her

U ain't financing…her

Please…

Shut the phuck up!

8). sprechgesang of love

Deep in the woods

Holding hands

Taking a walk

Along the river bank

Guessing at the horizon

At the beauty of the Sun rays

Beaming on two souls

Whose journey is about to begin

Deep in the woods

Holding hands

Seated on a rock

You can hear the echoes

Of beautiful whispers

Of new found love

Ricocheting from a distance

Deep in the woods

Holding hands

Walking back

The birds are chirping

The wind is ululating

Celebrating two souls

Whose love has just hatched

9) Long distance love

A kiss and the plane ascended

To overseas my studies to extend

With oaths and promises intended

Our lifetime relationship to defend

Phone calls and emails become the trend

The loneliness and distance to transcend

Flowers, gifts I could send

My world was hers to spend

But not long before I was dumbfounded

On June 9th of that weekend

With a voicemail that left me stranded

"To say that I love you is to pretend"

This message was hard to apprehend

My love she had begun to vend

Eloping with my best friend

The beginning of our relationship's end

This poem is not to offend

But solely for your heart to attend

My broken heart for you to mend

Our cherished relationship to defend

Two in one forever to blend

10) MINskirt

Miniskirt?

Or minus skirt?

Miniskirt

Where do you reach?

What do you preach?

Miniskirt

If my hands can reach

What law will they breach?

Miniskirt

Don't you think it's foul?

That you light desire in my soul?

Miniskirt

Is it unusual?

That I find you sexual

Why the fever pitch slit

Connecting at your split?

Miniskirt

How do you expect me to be strong?

Yet when you sneeze I can see your thong

Miniskirt

What of the visible panty line

That races my adrenaline

Miniskirt

Why assume the dress code of an infant

That causes a stunt in my pant

Miniskirt

Why don't you give me a warning?

To avoid the global warming

Miniskirt

Why do you excite my sword?

Even without uttering a word

Miniskirt

Aren't there ways you can dress casual

Without being sensual

Miniskirt

Or should I hope for the best

That in between I can taste

Miniskirt

Stop tempting my luck

If you know you can't let me pluck

Miniskirt

Please lengthen your height

To set my heart straight

Miniskirt

11) Always be my baby

To listen to their advice I may

But their opinions will not sway

No matter what barriers they lay

I won't let them stand in our way

Whatever the price I will pay

My love I promise shall stay

Don't mind whatever they say

You will always be my baby

Our love is an indelible badge

The world with hate to begrudge

Full of gossip and malice to lodge

With attempts to push us to edge

Beware of the poison they wedge

Their break up wish to dodge

My love for you I pledge

You will always be my baby

They are fence sitters waiting

For our drop

But their stones and curses

Shall flop

Two in one we shall cope

These valleys and hurdles

To hop

With an indomitable spirit

To the top

To remain united is our job

My love for you has no full stop

You will always be my baby

This poem I dedicate to arrest

Your uncertain fears to rest

As I keep you close to my chest

Your love to cherish and nest

My actions of love to attest

To the world from east to west

That forever I shall give you my best

You will always be my baby.

12). Dear Bikini

Loosely hang on the skin

You make my head spin

Bikini

You pass and leave me guessing

My eyes 360 chasing

Bikini

Why suggestively reveal

Yet mischievously conceal

Bikini

You are the only sexy sheriff

That always makes me stiff

Bikini

Are you sure you want me to discover

Whatever that lies undercover

Bikini

How do you expect me to be at ease?

When my mind you constantly tease

Bikini

Is yours a trap for felony?

By setting my head in agony

Bikini

Should I or should I not use a microphone

That the public is a no go zone

Bikini

In public your job you outreach

Your rightful place is in the beach

Bikini

Between nudity and beauty

What best defines your duty

Bikini

I bet you act as a fulcrum

If it's true or not is a conundrum

Bikini

Yours is the most coveted job

My wish list dream job you top

Bikini

In shops you hike the sells

In the sidewalks you top the tales

Bikini

Despite how small you are in size

The higher you pose a price

Bikini

You are my eyes favorite food

That leaves me in a curious mood

Bikini

How much is a VIP pass

To dine in the lower and upper class

Bikini

The truth is your amorous attire

Sets my manhood on fire

Bikini

Please heed to my confession and hide

Or else my fingers will run astride

Bikini

Not even sitting on a stack of bibles

Can help calm these sexually induced ripples

Bikini

How about if I play it kind

By requesting for your change of mind

Bikini

To increase your chest and hip length

For a brother to regain his strength

Bikini

Already I have some Vaseline lotion

With your little pink picture in motion

Bikini

Standing by the bathroom sink

muscles tense I cannot even blink

Bikini

To see me in high definition

Here is my free demonstration

Ouch!!!! i fear the condemnation.

13). Joanna give me hope

I

Will

Kill

And

Spill

Her blood

To fill

This

Emotional shell

That makes

Me

ill

I

Will

Kill

And

Spill

Her blood

To bill

This

Emotional debt

That is weighing

Me down

I

Will

Not

Kill,

This poem

Is just a

Skill

That I use

Like a

Pill

To release

Spill

My emotions

To enable me to cope

Not to take the rope,

Joanna give me hope

14). Touch you there

I wanna touch you there

Not physically but mentally

Peruse through your mind

with the gentle caress of a poetic muse

Discover the woman in you

and expose the treasures buried deeply within you

until it's not just u and me… but …WE.

I wanna touch you not with my hands but with words

Sensual words that will make you beg for me to touch you
physically to calm the embers ignited in more intricate places

Yes I wanna touch u there…

Deep down in your heart

15). The not yet born

Your mama is in pain

With considerable weight gain

My expectations are high

I wait with I sigh,

Each day draws you near

With breath sounds getting clearer

Great shall be the day

When your first cry shall beckon

Welcome to the world

To make you feel at home

I will recite you this poem

I will embrace you like my sword

And spoil you with my word

This poem writing to inherit

In poem writing to merit

Dear, my not yet born

Your skills I will horn

Your life will be unique

A Greek puzzle unanswered

In you I see a philosopher

A genius showstopper

The library will be your playground

Books and pens will be your toys

I will endear you to Chinua Achebe

And befriend you to Angelo Maya

Their knowledge to borrow

In their paths to follow

Dear, my not yet born

This poem is not a manual

But a secret cord from the usual

A reminder to brew with your enemies

But drink with your fathers

In you I see my shadow

A chip of the old pot

Promise son

That when my time is over

You will take this pen

And climb the tower

16). S.T.D

Why should I read the books?

When I have the looks

The professor only needs to flirt

And he will own my skirt

When spring break reaches

We shall elope to the beaches

I will cleverly attend a luncheon

With my distinguished anatomy surgeon

In the dim lights of neon

My ignorance he will bludgeon

Towards the semester end

He will remember the sensual bend

Despite my zero lecture attendance

He will grade me by the sexual dance

Proudly I will be crowned with a degree

By virtue of the sexual decree,

Behold I detest the dishonest imbalance

The root cause to academic decadence

That bores intellectual morons

Or call them half-baked graduates

Our professors I put to shame

To be ethical and take the blame

It behooves them to stop this game

Our education status to uplift its name

From sexually transmitted degrees

17). Amazing

Amazing is what I see

When you cross my path

Amazing is your wonderful ass

The way you wiggle it so nice

Amazing is my seductive charm

That amazingly you give me your number

Amazing is when you say

"Let's meet on a certain date"

Amazing for the first time

I at-least try not to be late

Amazing that at the end of the date

all roads lead to my house

Amazing is your intoxicating scent

When I carry you up the stairs

Amazing is your goddess body

When you start to strip

Amazing is the imminent connection

Underscored with passionate kisses

Amazing is how I feel

When u kneel before me

Amazing in my pants

When it starts to rise

Amazing is your facial expression

When I slap it on your forehead

Amazing is what you say

"Omg its 8 inches long"

Amazing are your oral skills

When you start to deep throat

Amazing is your gag reflex

when you start to cough

Amazing how you jam it back n forth

No Hollywood porn actress can match

Amazing is my favourite quote

"Tit for tat is a fair game"

Amazing is how you feel

When I glide my tongue on ya clit

Amazing is the taste in my mouth

When I lick n suck on ya lips

Amazing is the feeling you get

When my tongue squeezes through your walls

That you amazingly start to beg

"Please enter...me...and do me hard"

Amazing is when I flip u over

For that dog-style deepest penetration

Amazing is the rhythmic swing

Accompanied with powerful strokes

Amazing are ya slutty pleas

"Oh baby fuck me harder"

Amazing you start to push me back

As you can feel it gliding on ya cervix

Amazing are my beads of sweat

Trickling on ya booty providing more lubrication

Amazing are your chockfull moans

"Oh god I'm about to cum"

Amazing are ya pussy muscles

When they start to convulse

Amazingly your whole body starts to shake

Followed by resplendent pouts of cum

Amazing that our orgasms are in sync

As we all collapse in bed

........With an amazing story to tell

Of one amazing poem

18). Deeply in love

It's me and you

On a Sunday night

In a candlelit room

In pin drop silence

Holding hands

Sipping wine

It's me and you

Guessing at the window

At raindrops chanting

Down the window glass

To a lovers embrace

Of kisses flying

It's me and you

Standing at the window

Silhouettes gyrating

To the passionate flow

Of the whistling thorns

Brushing on the window

It's me and you

Immersed in sweat

To love notes whispered

Of soulful moans

To a Monday dawn

It's me and you

Feeling soar

Getting up the floor

To the piercing Sun-rays

Celebrating love birds

Who are deeply in love

19). Can you feel me?

Can u feel me?

Edging closer closing the gap

Can u feel me?

Rubbing against u emanating the heat

Can u feel me?

Running my fingers through ya hair

Can u feel me?

Kissing the back of ur neck n shoulder blades

Can u feel me?

Unfastening ya bra and cupping ur breasts

Can u feel me?

Kissing ya nipples n sucking them gently

Can u feel me?

Tracing kisses beyond ya navel

Can u feel me?

Gripping ya waist my lips on ya hips

Can u feel me?

My tongue slowing down taking a holiday on ya clit

Can u feel me?

Licking n sucking ya clit make it tick

Can u feel me?

Continuing my journey to the mouth of ya honeypot

Can u feel me?

Licking that opening in a circular motion

Can u feel me?

Tongue diving into ya honey pot

Nice n slow

Can u feel me?

All tongue submerged stirring ya honey pot

Mmm yummy!

Can u feel me?

As u squirt forth

Glowing my mustache with ya waters

Can u feel me?

20). U cheated on me

I gave u my world to own

But now my love u disown

I didn't know u a gold digger

Till ur pockets got bigger

It's sad that u blinded me with love

When I took u for an angel from above

U started to cheat behind my back

Deleting received calls to conceal the track

How could u fuck my best friend?

Yet swear it's not ur trend

My best friend unbuttons ur blouse

Right in my uptown house

Then u rush home to kiss my mouth

After kissing another man's south

U were a virgin I thought u the tricks

Now u riding other men's dicks

Do u expect me to take the pride

When they tell u "I love how u ride"?

Forget the flowers and candles

Behold the door I turn the handle

Please don't call my phone

I don't wanna hear ur voice or tone

21). Woman

Woman!

Without a dress

You are a temptress

Ready to impress

Woman!

In bed you are boneless

Your stunts on the mattress

Leave me speechless

Makes me confess

Oh my goodness!!

Woman!

You love it tireless

When I make you breathless

Making you to confess

"Oh!! My goodness"

Woman!

I love your madness

The way you express

Your emotions in excess

Just to suppress

A rumored mistress

22). I want you to feel me.

I want u to feel me

Feel my fire and desire

To host you in my penthouse suit

Feel my excitement and anticipation

To brawl and tear your thong

Feel my mahogany thighs

Framing you against the wall

I want you to feel me

Feel the craze of my crave

Of rubbing my skin against yours

Feel the beat of my heart

My chest heaving against yours

Feel the urge in my pants

Standing saluting your treasure

I want you to feel me

Feel my muscular arms

Hoisting u shoulder high against the wall

Feel my erotic tongue

Conversing with the tip of your clit

Feel the thickness of my lips

Nibbling sucking your clit

I want you to feel me

Feel my thirsty tongue

Gliding down your slimy ooze

Feel my gentle groove

Spreading apart your swollen lips

Feel the tip of my tongue

Making circles on your entrance

I want you to feel me

Feel my tongue diving deep

Making you hiss and piss(squirt)

Feel it back and forth

Patenting your inside with its warmth

Feel it caressing your tightness

Making your walls convulse

I want you to feel me

Feel me making you beg

"Please baby enter me now"

Beg me in mournful screams

"Baby please push it deep"

Beg me to increase the speed

"Baby please do it fast"

Beg for my intense strokes

"Oh baby I love it rough

23). Perfect storm

I can see myself kneeling

Just enjoying the feeling

My head deeply burrowed

Digging for the divine pleasure

From your coveted golden treasure

Your eyes roll within their sockets

Helplessly nudging me to stop

That I promise to after hitting the spot

My arms surrounding your waist

Firmly stretching you to the limit

A passion so strong to admit

As your nerves bulge with blood

To the building anxiety of the flood

A little bit of vanilla on your skin

And a little bit of Italian wine

Just to make your head to spin

As I celebrate and enjoy the feast

Licking the ice-cream from breast to breast

Tapping the wine streaming down your belly

Turning your thighs into jelly

Making you grasp and gasp for air

As though you are in an electric chair

My fingers quick to embrace

Caressing your spine with grace

Enjoying the twist and turns

As I wistfully whisper stories

Before we start burning calories

Imploring the best angle and side

Preferably from back with legs astride

Your knees deeply buried in the mattress

With your breasts caressing the sheets

Clapping at every stroke

Your bottoms dancing to the beats

Back and forth is the groove

The burning desire to disapprove

Keeping the tidal waves in motion

Of two souls colliding in action

Moving from wall to wall

In an ecstatic passionate embrace

"Yeah baby" so you speak

Your legs tightly lock

Slowly as I deep it to the rock

Feeling your juices flock

Then I know you are almost at the peak

And it's time to stop the clock

24). How will you like it.

How will you like it?

If I pushed you to the wall

Hands intertwined above shoulders

Kisses trailing down your neck

Flaming your shoulder blades

My tongue taking a Holiday on your breasts

Will you push me away with disgust?

Or will you push your nipples further into my mouth?

How will you like it?

If my tongue did errands on ya breasts

Licking each nipple at a time

Circling kisses from the plumb flesh to the tip

Just like drawing spokes on a wheel

Will you slap me and snap ya bra back on?

Or will you hold me by ears firmly to make sure I don't move?

How will you like it?

If I trailed kisses down ya navel

Further beyond your waist

My fingers racing to beat my tongue for your clit

Rubbing it gently to firmness

Like a bean pod in farmers market

Will you grab your thong from the doorknob and run away?

Or will you grab my fingers and push them deeper into your sex?

How will you like it?

If I carried you up against the wall and sat you on my shoulders

My tongue deeply squeezing through your convulsing walls of

Splendour

Making you squirm and hiss at its warm gentle penetration

Will you break an ankle by trying to jump off from my dirty
deeds?

Or will you close your eyes, stay still and let me get drunk off ya
oozing juices of eternal life?

How will you like it?

If I lowered you down

and bent u over against the wall

My right hand tugging on your hair

My left hand on ya clit rubbing it furiously

My 8 inch sword fully submerged in your honey pot

My rhythmic strokes syncing with your choking moans of pleasure

To trickling beads of sweat splashing on your lower back.

Will u run to the fridge for ice cubes?

Or will you push me back to the floor with determination to sit on my tree of sin and ride it to satsfucktion?

How will you like it?

Again if I flipped you over

To complete the job with my tongue

Licking your swollen lips inside out down to your slimy ooze

With the smacking noises of a dog lapping water from a bowl

Will you push me away with pleas of

"Please please stop baby I can't take it no more"?

Or will you push my header deeper into your lunch box

So that I can have this delicious buffet to multiple orgasms

How will you like it?

25). Do me

Strip me

Caress me

Kiss me all over

Take me higher it's u I need

Hold me

Squeeze me

Lower my thong

Unleash the dragon show me what u got

Finger me

Suck me

Lick me wet

Take ur time it ain't running away

Tie me

Whip me,

Spank me again

Kinky sex is all I need.

Gag me

Choke me

Pull my hair

Fuck me as though ur life depends on it

Slide it

Shove it

Stroke it to the hilt

Make this kitty your playground zone

Harder

Faster

Deeper please

Make me cum like a fountain spring

26). I wanna

I wanna

Stare into ur eyes n provoke ur desire

I wanna

Pull u closer n hold u nearer

I wanna

Kiss ur lips n light ur fire

I wanna

Caress ur skin n take u higher

I wanna

Nibble ur nipples make em hard

I wanna

Touch ur lust make u sigh

I wanna

Pool the hit within ur thighs

I wanna

Make u sweaty hot n bothered

I wanna

Touch that spot

Kiss that spot

Lick that spot

Hit that spot -until u squirt

I wanna

Make u feel like a puddle of melting candle wax

I wanna

Crash ur waves till u fall asleep

I wanna

Make u scream "please don't stop"

I wanna

Make u hate me because I just stopped.

Back & Forth by Deep Rivers & Lyrical Poet

27) The journey.

D-We started this journey not knowing

Words from deep constantly flowing

L-a journey not defined by love, it being boundless as the show

But exhibited by literary lines, echoing impacts beyond the minds horizon

D-Your scent arouses what I kept locked away

Now I sit my heat you invade

L-I let my affection stir the cauldron of ur emotions

Flaming ur hearts fire n desire to crave for me

D-Reaching down into the most intimate of places

Lips travel as your thickness expands my spaces

L-u pull me closer to do a reconnaissance study of the sensual vase that desires to be inscribed with an eight inch pen. My pen-is seductive, it stands drooling at ur thighs as our hips merge welcoming miss kitty n dick for the impending grand coalition.

D-Mounting you for the ride of a lifetime

Your body responds back arched hard as a dime

L-thighs hugging , organs kissing, u bore ur flesh into my pen, the marvelous sight of that diamond pen penetrating ur flesh spelling a new world Order of ecstasy up ur walls into ur insides.

D-Slow then fast the beating in tune

Like the fresh flowers in bloom.....

L- Our silhouettes dance in darkness back n forth like two marionette puppets in the hands of an erotic prankster.

Bodies glistening with sweat Mark the epitome of pleasure iced with animalistic noises of two lovers hitting a crescendo of a good love making session.

D-As the explosion goes on for eternity or so it seems

As I calm slowly waiting for what you hold for me

Mind moving fast as my body is still waiting anticipating for the next rush

L-Heat in the air surrounded by the scent of ecstasy

The strong presence of you all around or is it my fantasy

D-My pen scribes only to you as my body drifts under your spell

My wish to forever live the moment of you and I

Creating orgasms that make us one and scream for the sky

L-All this from the lips

From your hips

And the amazing trip

That you create deep in my soul

D-I wait patiently for your next move

28) Home cuming

L-Cuming home to Empty seats

The fridge is dry

Where is my baby?

D- You ask where is my baby

Did you stop and wonder how many times I had to ask

Wondering where or who you were hidden behind the mask

L-Another lonely night

To gaze at the stars

The one I love is not in sight

D- So many lonely nights that I spent alone

waiting patiently by the phone

Hoping that I would cross your mind

Grabbing the phone all I got was a dead line

L-I toss and turn in my lonely bed

From wall to wall embracing my pillow

The comforting piece that soon you will be home

D-just as I get a grip on my thoughts I drift

Not allowing my mind to continuously roam

I know Deep in my heart that you will come home

Replacing all doubt wrapped safe in your arms

L-My pillow is drenched with solitary tears

My sheets are stained from

Whipping fears

Tell me the number, how many years?

D- And although we both travel this path

You should understand the volume of my wrath

Remember you experience now what I have for so many years...

but I'm still glad you came home....

29). Words that flow.

Deep: The words that flow from me to you

Cause and effect at times taboo

Lyrical: Convincing sweet penetrating words

That light up ur erotic shores of yonder

Deep: You entered a place deep and yet undefined

My mind you took across all erotic lines

Lyrical: A place where angelic

boys had long feared to tread

That my words of passion feared not to run

Deep: The heat that stirs from the words that flow

Reach the depths of my ignited soul

Lyrical: Infectious heat that warms up even the Siberia of your body

Bringing to life your unexploited love

Deep: Sensations created

Desires elated

Temptation of an erotic style

The flow that fulfills mile after mile

Lyrical: wordsmith's words that wakens your passions

Fantasies provoked

Scenes crafted

Sins committed

Deep: Thighs squeezed tight

Eyes tighter

The emotions float higher and higher

Lyrical: yearning desires

Burning fires

Reflected in waves of overwhelming emotions

Deep: This all from the response to your flow

Never to stop on the heat from below

Lyrical: glowing words meant to blow

These seeds of seduction

In your heart I sow

30). Cold raindrops

Deep:

Cold raindrops that refresh the fallen sun

Heat turned down

As we prepare for round two

Touches that entice

Soft whispers trail my spine

Lips locked intertwined

Hips sway

Gyrate to a hidden beat

Only in my mind

Carefully playing an erotic tune

Flowers return to full bloom

All from the raindrops...

Lyrical:

Rainbow reflection outside the bedroom window

Seven colors spell my love for u

The tiny droplets of rain on the window start to dance

The more I gaze into ya burning emerald eyes

The fiery passion flames my heart

It takes two to tangle I pull u closer

U hold me dearly and close your eyes

As my wedge cracks through your honey pot

Your soft moans turn into background music

Neck biting and finger burrowing take me higher

The simmering heat begins to rise

The droplets on the window turn to sweat

I pick you up and hold u in my palm

Roll my tongue and blow into the glass

Watch with awe as you bloom into a flower.

A beautiful rose that wakes me up from up

Up from my grandiose dream.

31). Next move

Deep:

Contemplating my next move

Move of a lifetime with life at stake

I give

I live

I love and I work hard

All my cards all in

This battle destined to win

Consuming thoughts

Stirring deep sensations

Yearning love from the depth of my soul

Cards all in

Destined to win

Traveling through time with winning in my heart

Nothing to distract

As the battle of the heart is won

Lyrical:

Love rages -daggers drawn

Curtains drawn -eyes closed

Feelings fighting -love is blind

Love is the prize -hearts competing

Emotions referee- my heart is lost

Lost to a stranger -a familiar thief

Who thinks my heart- is hers to chief

To steal to guard -without my brief

She is done it in style- to close the deal.

With gusto and zeal -looking so real

Tonight she triumphs -my heart is gone

To a love resort -where love belongs

32) Divine Love

D-You control my every move with your lips

I sway I tilt, my hips gyrate

Nothing I do to myself feels this great

L-my lips of splendor on your feminine folds

Caressing provoking tectonic movements

No comparison to ur self-loving nights

D-Shivering beneath you as my juices flow

Wanting and needing more than you know

L-pussy tremors lyrically manufactured

No holds(holes) barred let the honey ooze

D-You approach me slow the heat I feel

Whispering for me to just lie still

L-your body is canvas in my tapestry bed

To perfect my eroticism in a state of inertia

D-Heart racing blood pumping through my veins so fast

Wanting you needing you to mount this ass

L-no fuss or haste let me wet my pen

Picasso at work let me paint ur interior with cream

D-My treasure wet and hot needing your touch

The lips the hips needing so much

L-u got the needs I got the supply

Time is of the essence let me rock ur boat.

D-You enter your tongue wet and so hot

Tasting me licking me lots and lots

L-on and on like Michael Jackson

Stopping not till u get enough.

D-I feel a cool breeze from where I don't know

Replaced with the heat as your chocolate stick grows

L-my pen+is hard like a blacksmiths nail

Grows in ur honey pot making it glow

D-Slow strokes going at a steady pace

Hitting my spot from the look on my face

L-walls expand my member to accommodate

As I stroke u with precision to paradise blues.

D-The rhythm so smooth you can write your own song

The loving I been waiting for oh so long

L-the wood has been torched

Let the embers glow

As my stream drains into your oceanic floor

33). Hidden passion

Deep:

The words that describe the inner me

To hear my silence

To heal my unknown violence

Escape to a place of tranquility

You are my fantasy

Safe in your arms

Caressed with your charm

Heat causing a sensuous alarm

Wet kisses that bring peace

Soft as lambs fleece

A touch that creates

A seductive state

All from my erotic mate

Embarking upon a mission of thrill

The thickness I take at will

Stroking me as I stroke you

Enveloped into an orgasm so brand new

Lyrical:

The inner voice is my words

That unravels ur unknown violence

Soothing your unfulfilled fantasies with indescribable passion

Passion reflected in my fashion

When I carry you with my strong gym trainer arms

And slam ur back against the kitchen fridge

My thick pen scraping through ur yearning walls of sweetness

Penetrating to the hilt of ur honey comb

Answering ur quest for a thrill with a perfect drill

Ur honey sipping through the fleshy pages of eroticism

As me and you connect in these field of erotica

Saving more flavor for the next poem

34). Search

Deep: On the prowl for the one that can please

Causing my juices to flow with ease

Lyrical: look no further I'm here at ur disposal, your source of juices to stir and tap

Deep: See I search and found none that can satisfy

The desires that are beyond the sky

Lyrical: remove the veil from your eyes to see, the freak in me who can take you places, beneath and beyond the sexual horizon.

Deep: My desire for the one that brings me orgasm after orgasm

Body trembles constant spasms

Lyrical: Your raw desires are peripheral I crave, I can do one plus more ur passions to enchant

Deep: Tongue that explores

With a dick that I adore

Adventure to the hidden door

Lyrical: adventure at noon adventure in the morning my tongue is the sequence my dick is the series, u do the math from the bed to the floor.

Deep: Hidden from those who know not how to please

Constant upset as they all are a tease…

Lyrical: Ur slippery slope is error to my reputation, give me room and your tune shall change

Deep: Continue my search for the one who can please

Lyrical: message delivered I ain't no tease, I'm here to please at ur beck n call

35). Having it all

Deep: When will I have all that I can get

Loving from the hills to the valley

The ultimate orgasm that leaves me vibrating for more

Can you deliver?

Or shall I continue my search

For the one whose value is beyond worth

Strokes that give

Trying to relive

All that I am

Judgment I don't give a damn

I desire the most

Searching coast to coast

Can you give all that you boast???

Lyrical: I'm a timeless lover who boasts not

I don't speak for the world but it does for me

They who been with me can preach you my strength

On cold nights I serve it hot

Till u drip sweat like torrents of rain

In summer nights when u feeling fatigued

I massage you with strokes' with a condensation effect

Woman of desire come to me

No need to wander from coast to coast

Cum to me let's make a toast

36). Open Wide

Deep: Open wide for all to see

The feelings that flow from you to me

Lyrical: arms stretched the door is open

From sphere to sphere even the galaxy is my witness

Deep: feelings that hold my deepest thoughts

Allowing all of me to show as the emotions go

Lyrical: feelings welling for you to bath in

Tenderized heart your emotions I will sponge

Deep: You have opened a once closed door

You have stripped my clothes thrown on the floor

Lyrical: just for you my dearest love

Naked to the nerves let the feelings flow

Deep: completely exposed for you to really see

Will you continue to tease or complete me?

Lyrical: eyes have no curtains I'm taking center stage

My eyes traversing grazing on ur curves

no teasing factor I will more than please

Deep: Heart warm and tender ready for what comes

Wanting and needing so much to make us one

Lyrical: the response is mutual give me ur hand

Let's tango in love to ur favorite band

37). Fear

Deep: Fear of the unknown

Wielded heart

Heat rising

And yet I'm all alone

Lyrical: imaginary fear

Pale or real

That my heart radiates

To light ur interior

Deep: Enthralled by the scent of you

Captured by all that you do

Lyrical: the scent that lingers even after I'm gone

Wafting ur senses

Into inescapable fences

Deep: And I ask myself

What is this spell?

Only my heart can tell

Lyrical: mysterious binding spell

Unknown to u, but ur heart

Comprehends "love is the word"

Deep: Whispers in the night

Desires feel so right

Lyrical: backdrop silence punctuated

By whispers

But broken by the surface tension of desires

Deep: But am I wrong

Wanting you for oh so long

Lyrical: Lose not sleep for I'm urs for keeps

The wait maybe long but it's worth the reward

Deep: Kisses that leave me breathless

Urges that cause me to be restless

All craving your simple caress

Lyrical: I shall flood u with kisses

Of life

Simple caress n kisses that resuscitate ur love

Deep: Am I wrong

Wanting and needing for so long

As I continue to play the same old song

Lyrical: ur right in all aspects to sing the song of love

Let the lyrics flow through ur veins

Knowing that the want n need is mutual

Deep: Your my alpha and omega in this song of love…I need you….

Lyrical: Not more than I want u too

38). Melody of the mountains

Lyrical: In my heavenly garden of splendor

I'm seated with a beautiful woman

Her sexy eyes of passionate conduit

Begs me with mastery affection

To swim her through the erotic waters

I take her to the

Melody Mountains

To feed her craving affection

She opens her lips of seduction

And sits on my tree of sin

Deep: As I sit on the tree of sin

My body allows my fire to burn again and again

My eyes speak of the pleasure you give

Causing my body to relive

Relive the deepest of desires

As you continue to take me higher

The strokes that cause sensations

The lips that bring gratification

The grip that shows dedication

To all that is within

From the moment I sat on the tree of sin

39) Dreams

Deep:

It is not always as it seems

My deepest thoughts trapped in my dreams

Fighting for reality

My love is more than a technicality

Craving what was once a practicality

Now exposed my sexuality

To give and take

Avoiding all mistakes

Desires run wild

That once sheltered child

Whirlwind of emotion

Hypnotized with your potion

Emerging from the darkness

Only to be drowned in you…

Lyrical:

The dreams to be sated and satisfied by the one who u hanger for

The one u only gets to hear of him

In erotic tales

Mystified by the truth of his existence

Like a tempest in a tea cup

U nudges him into

An exploratory erotic journey

Where the u in u gets intimate with the he in him

In ink n paper pen-tration

Arousing feelings that leave u drowned

In self-indulgence once again to

Seek ur lost heart in him

40). Speaking to my soul

Deep:Can the eyes that I stare into speak to my soul?

Telling a story of desire, passion a rhythmic flow?

Lyrical: Can ur eyes accommodate the overflowing love that my eyes refracts into urs?

Endless love to last you a month of Sundays and beyond

Deep:Do they hold secrets of lust?

Or are they the eyes my heart can trust

Lyrical:These eyes can hold more than told

Even ur deep fiery secrets of lust and thrust

Deep:See I search for the man that is true

To take me places that I never knew

Lyrical:Doubt me not to take u places

My heart is your gps, type ur destination of choice

Deep: Strokes long

> Glide after glide

> A dick that definitely provides

Lyrical: A journey of unwavering strokes

> Into ur destination,

> Of certified strokes that jells ya desires

Deep:Lips wet

Licking here

Sucking everywhere

Lyrical:Swollen lips leaking wet

Coated with glistening

Seductive nectar

Deep:Are these the eyes that speak to my soul

That will allow my passion to continue to grow

Lyrical:Penetrating look, doubts erased

Come to me, your love to grow

Grow to the height of explosion

Deep: Are these the eyes that are more than a notion......

Lyrical:Promise is a debt this I know

Lyrical eyes never lie,

They here to cast their spell of love

41). To Satisfy

D-Wanting a man to please me

Never leaving me wanting for more

L-Application I lodge for consideration

Your crave to blaze to satisfaction

D-Hell does this exist or is it left at the door

My sexual appetite greater than most

L-I know I can bite more than I can chew

Welcome to lyrical's pleasure dome.

D-My sexual appetite is feared coast to coast

The man that I'm seeking must have what it takes

L-Seek not into the skies

The appetite you boast I can toast

D-To tame this pussy a lot is at stake

My pleasure box is waiting for you

L-Behold I have the love paraphernalia

Your ticking love box to tame

D-The man that can make me say damn you are true

See the problem at hand is so small to me

L-In my pleasure dome your wish is my command

Your craving desires define me

D-I want the man that can fuck me freely

Not once not twice three times is a start

L-Your begging is to be past tense

Once we embark on the fucking spree

D-Fuck me, suck me like a piece of fine art

Once we are finish the game never ends

L-with me you will be screaming

"please stop-I need a breathing break"

D-Hell I want the man that can say let's fuck all over again

L-The keys to my pleasure dome I surrender

The remote to my groove is at your disposal

Let me know when to stop

42) Stuck on you

Deep:

Stuck in my own thoughts longing for you

Asking over and over what do I do?

To walk away

With hell to pay

Or do I simply say

I want to stay

Tackling the thoughts of you

Seductive, I want you

Sensual, I need you

Stimulating, I crave you

All the erotic thoughts that flow

From my mind body and soul

You and I to complete this task

As we remove all our masks

Exposed to one another

Nothing to hide as we enjoy beneath the covers

Lyrical:

Nowhere to go u belong to me

Your body your soul belongs to me

Your craves your thoughts belong to me

I'm your master craftier the only one to know

The one who pulls ur hearts strings

Leaving u no room to escape from my love imprisonment

The love that encompasses all your spheres

Fomenting your fantasies

Tormenting your moves

The master puppeteer to whose love you bow

Who understands you emotionally as well physically?

He who whips u erotically

Yet consoles u romantically

Come to me and tent in my heart.

Ms. Creoleness

She was born in New Orleans, LA with a passion for therapy through inkfilled strokes. She has allowed her pen and pad to become one while bringing all of her joys, hurts, admissions and sexual desires to many hearts and minds..Her Creological Wordly Meteorite may require you to ponder on your own lustful discretions so "Bring your Own Wett Wipes."

"Be mindful of the words expressed and the actions portrayed for anyone can view you as a Role Model.."

1) Untitled

The emptiness feels like a canvas

As if your lips never touched me

Listening to R.Kelly's "Go Low"

I know exactly how freaky I want to be

I want to climb and ride with a watermelon taste

Knowing this Jolly Rancher Pussy is all over your face

I want to be mentally fucked from your tongue mingled of juices

Tequila, Corona, Dasani, I don't want any excuses

Lay me down and feel the heat between my legs

It's like being consumed by lava but I want to beg

For the explosion of moisture like a Water Country Slide

No need for kneepads or bibs for the delectable 69

So excited like the NFL Draft

Rubbing my clit with your hands but longing to be stabbed by your shaft

Picking positions not players for us to be buck

Thrusting, sweating and word spinning 1st round luck

Pull it out; I want to see it milking and its worth

Legs and arms quiver, I need a restart

By the blink of an eye all I saw was a shirt

I was hit hard like a goalie that has missed the puck

So this is what it is to be a victim of mind phuck

2) Poetry

The thoughts of your hands had me controlled

As if I was a flower in a lake waiting for mold

Conversations no longer necessary I was told

Warrior romantic experience I was shown

Loved like a geisha but admired like a centerfold

Amazed how my limbs spread like a tree welcoming a humming bird

Imagined being sensually eaten like the plumpest yard bird

Harmonizing of angels, I thought I heard

All that was muffled was a tiny single word "Turn"

Used a theory of happiness through someone's eyes

Passionately searching for a lost spirit between my thighs

Mind, heart and soul preferred to personalize

But the invisible area had me eulogized

My spontaneity finalized, materialized and sabotaged

My inner being but mesmerized by his advertise

Meant to be the electricity of the sounds on the phone

Had thoughts of epiphanies through the walls in my home

Inspired but frightened from our possible sexual tones

Of you inside of me like a New Orleans Superdome

Listening to Duke Ellington playing trombone

Found myself kneeling at the cathedral praying in Rome

Saying "Help"

Me to stop the weakened knees by your song

Mentally shaped like an oblong

Light as a feather but higher than Cheech and Chong

In tuned like a kindergarten ABC sing-along

But lost like pieces of Mahjong

Speaking for survival to stay strong

In my quest to do wrong

Our first encounter can't be accidentally

Placed in our stars for a forced compatibility

Passion delivered with such high velocity

With possible affinity

Need a helmet for your coach ability

Essence from eruptivity but taste for only my recipe

Used all my sky miles to embark cross country

Second thoughts of being numbered on your registry

Your swag and smells speaks to my entry

Platinum and oxygen helps keep the chemistry

You being my Ranger guided by this forestry

What is going on, look what has happened to me

Damn, the love and life of erotic poetry.

3) First Encounter

I want to fuck the life into your dreams

Knowing you feel about me that way makes things really absurd

In my heart I shouldn't touch what has been joined by His Word

Things happen for a reason you must learn

If I am truly a queen, your wife's feelings I must be concerned

The word was only, "Hello"

But mentally I imagined my pussy had his glow

With skill, precision and harmony to start a slide show

Like the Three Little Pigs, huffing and puffing, knocking my sugar walls shallow.

But my clit played like a violin

Oh Shit!!! I am in fuck mode again

Struggling but determined to find the lambskin

Ripping through my thighs like a sign saying "Come in"

The unveiling of my clothes, had my guide foreclosed

Sexuality x3 exposed

Amazed how quickly your manhood rose

As your arms slowly caressed my hips

Face slipped and said,"Ummm", to my lower lips

Sensual kisses as my boat begin to drip

Shocked not to witness a lunar eclipse

Let's what is underneath my skirt

Be your ultimate flirt by lusting over me like a pervert

For my strawberry gelatin dessert

Let's play a game of Taste or Dare

Since your head action is beyond compare

My turn to show you a Karma Sutra affair

In my mind I heard, "I want to suck your pussy through your asshole"

Looker sweeter than candy and probably thicker than a jelly roll

Put this cream in a can and sell it to Dole

Only thing I wanted was for him to be naked and pose

Fuck this, "Hey I want you to tickle my throat with your dick"

Pulsating muscles hitting my tongue to do tricks

Beyond ready for you to get inside

So don't let this pin cushion pussy pass you by.

My fantasy needs rehabilitation

From this sexual gratification

Sprung from his lick and dicktation,

Feeling sideways like a bee with severe salivation

Then he turned to me and said, "Ma'am I see you staring and I really appreciate the admiration, but let's start with a simple conversation "Hello".

4) IV

Your arms welcome me in like the rays

Of love to embrace from all despair

Lying beside you to eliminate my blues and grays

To give me the affection beyond compare

Your touch sends my word in a spiral

Searching the left and right side of my brain for approval

Of the scenery of butterflies in an aero dynamical

Design to beautify, mystify and coincide our clothing removal

"Okay Fuck That, Look!"

I want to be fucked into a coma

So I can stop experiencing this uncontrollable ache

My pussy and your dick is the best aroma

And just looking, I know it is as juicy as a Ruth Chris Steak

I want to taste and be tasted

Like the Hot Sign on Krispy Kreme

Do it with ease, admiration and starvation

Until my thongs are hanging from the seam

From the dance of your tongue, damn the acceleration

Celebration, demonstration and cognitive operation of my body's assassination

My fragile places explode like an atomic bomb

That the neighbors would tune in and watch

Me on top, you on top, me on top, maybe you behind

Shit the temperature is rising; damn you found my "G" spot

Get deeper into my cave with each step of penetration

Skin blended into one with each inch brings orchestration

Imagination and lots of hallucination

How can I show this Poet what he just can't see?

Wish me luck because he has no idea what he is doing to me

But I am going to get his attention, Damn me nervous, can't be

Here it goes, "Excuse me; I want to feel and drink you intravenously".

5) Do You?

My hands want to feel me

But my loins want to blend within you inside of me

Slowly pulling you closer

Hoping to give myself freely

Do you?

Legs in the air, head in the chair

Hula hoop hips, wanna see, Truth or dare?

Dick is so inviting, I can pull my own hair

Do you want?

I want to feel my cream escaping

My walls through anticipation

You see, I need that pulsating, captivating, illustrating, straight fuck making

Do you want to?

I desire you to be my motivator, dominator

My down right pleasure sedator

My admiration for you influences my masturbation with enormous saturation

Fuck me so hard, will be like creating history

Having me is your personal Big Bang Theory.

Do you want to cum with me?

6) One question

Lay me down on the bed

I'll get on top of you

Wrap your arms around me

Legs wrapped around your back

Feeling my heat between my legs

Getting warmer and harder

Feeling it, rubbing against my peach

Our tongues intertwined, dancing in each other's mouth

Sucking.....hmmmmmmm

I want you to slide down my pants

and enjoy the smell of my pussy getting hot

Panties soaked with each movement

Lips engorged and swollen

waiting for your mouth to cover it

Suck the clit making that circular motion that I like

Licking back and forth

Back and forth with the tip

Listening to the sucking sounds from enjoying my juicy peach

As I lay back holding my legs

You start to lick up and down my thighs

Sucking every piece of morsel of my flesh

You lift my hips higher

Sticking your tongue into my pussy

Deeply feeling my juices run all down your face

You roll me onto my stomach

Letting your tongue between my cheeks

You start to tongue fuck my asshole over

and over

and over again

Rubbing my clit with your hand

Your dick is welcomed into my tight wetness

I buck against it

Rocking back and forth

Feeling all of you inside of me

My lips take hold and milking it for all

You reach over and grab my hips

With one hand, thrusting as you go deep and slow

You feel my cum drip down your dick

As you continue to bash this pussy for more

You pull it out and admires its layers of juices

So I greedily start licking, sucking and slurping it off

Damn these pears were sweet.....

Your balls are now in my mouth..HMMMMMMM

I turn around, get on my knees and

You gently and softly introduce it to my asshole

But I can go slow until I can feel E-V-E-R-Y inch inside of me

I bounce and rock against you

Moaning and cooing

I spread my cheeks so you can have a better view

Your balls slapping against my cheeks

You grab my hair as you start to

Fuck me deeper

Harder

Thrusting inside of me

I rub my clit because I know this orgasm will wake up wolves.

You kiss my neck, sliding your tongue in my ears, intriguing my earlobes

Baby, I want it in my pussy

We kiss as passionately as we roll over

But now it is you who is on his back

I slide that thick cock inside while letting you admire the scenery

Legs spread

My hands around your neck, slowly choking you

Until

We both cum…

Baby, I am so sleepy

Did you really miss me?

one more thang

Who has been getting my dick...?

7) I fell for you

I think I am falling for you through subtle keystrokes

My keyboard is no longer an empty rectangular shell

Just being consumed with smiley faces, hearts and enters

As my poetic junkie, I don't care who you tell

Your voice reminds me of different fonts and styles

With each fingertip my plans change to take a chance

By awakening me from a dream with love and potential

To admire avatars' movements of our shadow's dance

I know I am falling for you when my heart melts with every picture and status

Understanding that you are my destiny

From my skin to your face

See, I who have nothing....you simply elevate me

Your eyes smile at me without hearing a word

I can sense your kisses with chills down my spine

It lifts the beats through my lungs to be close to yours

Thanks to the universe, our stars have aligned

I fell for you through the anticipation of love

That was as smooth as the calmness of the seas

Separating your actions which revolved without metaphors

Which the sounds of cum was heard and tasted within me

You completed all communication of our mixture

Without discretion, separation or even penetration

I appreciate you for accepting my request of uncertainty

That constantly has my mental capacity fueled from verbal
ejaculation.

I want to fall again.....

8) Your Pleasure

My pussy is tighter than your hands in surgical gloves

I want to be fucked; we can wait to make love

I want to feel higher than the heavens above

Transformed to an angel, naw I want to be that dove

The one that is mystified and kinky but some afraid to speak of

Spread my legs like the rivers and streams

To be nasty is beyond the extreme

To practice and tryout as the starting player on my team

Just put me on your microphone like Raheem

DeVaughn or devour your travels to collect per diem

Feeling so good that I want to see you cum upstream

Hopefully enough is left for seconds to redeem

So I can taste some of your supreme pineapple whipped cream

I can make you feel better than anything written by Zane

Fuck me so hard until I become the beat of your jugular vein

No need for romance, strawberries or even champagne

Your mind will be twisted like a sandstorm in Bahrain

I am more addicted than chocolate, nicotine or even cocaine

Have you hungry for me like you smoked a thick Mary Jane

My sugar last longer than pussy filled candy cane

Being spiritual connected or on your knees like you are being ordained

When you're inside I want to hum and whistle

Fuck me so hard until cum leaks from my bone gristle

With my fruit and your cock, we can drink some outstanding fruit cocktail juices

We will engage in role playing like you are in a house of prostitution

Looking for ways to graduate in this sex educational institution

Moving moon and stars like a fuckable Karma Sutra evolution

While prepping my pussy like it was the last meal before your own execution

Hopefully, you can grasp the concept of the word that I speak

For I know that the body is a temple and it's priceless like an antique

If headboard breaking is something that you seek

I can suck and swallow but you got to make me quaff.

9) I See Us

I have awakened from another

Fulfillment of my eyes and

I see us

Never to share the same feelings

But I see us

Two seeds thrown in the ground

Covered with soil reaching from the earth

Not for assistance through the process

Just to bloom within this garden of emotion

Left side of this garden is dirt

Never touched by water

Right side is a beautiful spread of white roses

In the middle is just...Us

As our roots grown and fast for air

Tiny flower is seen from the world

One

Singular

Individual

Not spectacular but deep within its own beauty

We are amazed how the roots get thicker

Through the seasons of uncertainty

Our words viewed like grass in the cracks in a precious landscape

We are in the same dirt

Sharing the same patch

Still unable to realize the strength without our soil

My roots will always touch yours

Allow the few drops of moisture

From my presence to enhance your soul for air

Our connection is deeper than an imaginary core

Let me hold onto your left side

For your troubles, cares and concerns

You can hold on to my right side

For compassion, empathy, trust and tears

We are still in the same path of dirt

Reaching from the earth for air

And afraid of how

We see Us…

10) One Aboard

Slurping your dick like the last pour of a Banana Slurpee

16oz cup filled from pure satisfaction and body of fantasy

A ticket has to be issued to ride, bring your thought to my gate

There is no line, or complaining, once aboard nothing is at stake

As you take a seat, smell the ripeness of this fruit

Dreaming about being amusingly sucked

Try to restrain from the passionate urge

Of feeling the breathing growing intensely

The anticipation of the twisting, turning, horizontal and vertical submission en route

Has you sweating and rising and we haven't achieved full throttle

This is real; I can feel you getting high

For you to love the adrenaline of services I provide

I will do it so good; you'll beg to go for faster and higher

Remember 1 ticket is all you need to be mine

I am not overconfident or cocky just want you to be comfortable inside

And this *Creologically* real

You will scream internally from the suspense but externally

Your body wants to scream

Letting your physical lust rise and peak

Allowing this ride to make you weak

I repeat, make you weak

As we entangled in my cloud filled satin sheets

My definition is different when it applies to stimulation

Because on this ride you need a better relation

Of achieving a superb sexual gratification

With my ride called Pussy Infiltration

You will give yourself to me naturally

Not virtually of course unconditionally

As you throw your hands up

Head back and scream

Viewing a concrete rose in a complex jungle from above

Love to hear you bringing spirituality into the reality

As you yell for E.T to come home

Lay all of your worried and sexual tension on me

By allowing your mind and body

To release in this *Creolastic* Ecstasy.

11) Send

In the day of conversation to you I want to be

When alone, your last text seems to comfort me

The tingling between my inner thighs become a lasting sea

The encounter vibrates around my nipples, feeling

Something, squeezing my legs a little tighter

Feeling you inside just lingering in my head

This is my greatest opponent and I am not a fighter

I can't help but imagine the day, wind and rhyme, what do I do?

I am not a match of what I feel, victim of my own voodoo

Taste of your lips, skin, breathing in my ear, as my nails gracefully in your back

Need you in my softest place, our love and passion would never lack

Yes, sliding between my thighs allowing the drip within my inner being

Sensual moisture glistening to my mouth, disbelief of what you are seeing

I want to command with this grand finale, with a special treat up my sleeve

I promise to be gentle, take my time and baby be sure to breathe

Release in and out of sounds of enjoyment slipping in my mouth with a passionate motion

Having a baby shower in my throat like the smoothest, warmest of lotion

Grip my locs and touch the deepest part of the throat in relief

Sorry baby, this encounter will not be brief

Again, positioning myself on your throne

Be prepared for hours for heavens will hear our moans

This is the time, reason and rhyme

The last text said I love you and it tickled my spine

I love you too for accepting me through rain, sun and wind

I can't wait to be in your arms and be fucked...Guess I better press

Send

12) Three n One

Let's be the nursery rhyme Jill and Jack

Holding on while you climb this hill from the back

Keep one Timberland on to prevent the fall and that's a fact

Fort the underwater fishing Mr. Cousteau, Jack

I am gonna fuck the vowels out of da alphabet

Rehearsing and spitting like Run DMC on cassette

Yeah a classical moment of scenes not to forget

My pussy aroma embedded in the seats in your Little Red Corvette

Like speed and adrenaline afterwards for an Atlantic Ocean Sweat

That only thing revealed is my naked lovely silhouette

While my lips on your dick like a perfect mouth on a clarinet

Don't be alarmed, you can have your turn, don't be upset

For the juices can flow or should I say juices beget

The sexual doo wop for this one time duet

To maintain the ultimate Cumsational threat

And we haven't even fucked yet

I want to fuck you into an embryo

Feeling my insides as you release would seem like birth

Hold on tight to my worldly meteorite

But how else can I explain my sexual worth

You see there are three to me but don't be confused

All of them have talents but aren't always being used

Wishing for ways we can behave by you feeling all of my senses

Afterwards you will always smell our sexual incenses

We can change our appearances to set any mood

Something's have to be a surprise I have come to conclude

Adrina is the conservative, reserved but sweet one

Who enters the bedroom for relaxation not for fun?

For her to be misunderstood or crushed and then she is done

Can appear cold but mature and never needs a dry run

Alexis is the chick to go over and beyond

The mountains and horizons to achieve that bond

Beware because Adrina keeps her caged for only you

Yes, the hunger of dick from mouth to pussy is true

Time and place is no longer an issue

Always on the menu

From appetizer to main course and will even dessert you

Alexis can have a mouthful without question or concern

She is there to please, sucking slowly like watching butter churn

Slowly swallowing like a Kiwi Quencher Smoothie

Another reason for many positions with this fuckery

Feeling so goof make you run and climb a tree

From this junglefied pussy or should I say this erotic monkey

I want the cum to leak from the cartilage in my knee

To see how intense I am into you and you are into me

Fuck me so hard until my tubes come untied

From our cursive strokes you will reach altitude and a high tide

Kinky or freaky whatever you call it, just keep it bonafide

Now that I have accomplished masturbation of your mind

I want one leg in my pussy until you think its quicksand and you're
sinking

Being so far in your thoughts until I want to fuck what you are
thinking

This poetic arousal is real and every change she will outdo

The previous time shared but this pussy isn't for passing through

I just want you to experience your dick having déjà vu

Check your keychain cause to unlock this *Creolastic* beast, it could
be you

Last is I may be twisted but don't misunderstand

Adrina will ask and patiently wait for you to be her man

But Alexis will pull your pants down and suck on demand

The goal is ultimate pleasure while touching her lymph gland

Creoleness wants to spit on this vocal dick and here I stand.

13) Another Dream

Taste of my lips

Maybe down to my cheeks

Tongue gliding down to the back of my neck

Fingers checking to see if I am wet

Shoulder kisses cuffing my breast

Tongue grazing my nipples

Sucking its erectness

Taking it in your mouth

Caressing its roundness

Grabbing my tight ass

Gripping and opening my thighs

Jogging your tongue down my navel

To the center of my clit

Licking until it starts to throb

Sucking my pussy till I start to grab

Losing your face in my center

Pulling my pelvis to be still

Squeezing both of my assets

Until I start to moan

Fucking me with your tongue

Searching for air through wet follicles

Tasting my walls and sucking my lips

Till I cum hard, wide open, you can hear my deepness

No ordinary penetration can prepare me for this

To hold your arms while enjoying you taste me

When it's my turn it will seem like eternity

This type can be spiritual as well as magical

For the reality of the mind

Touch from the back of your neck down to your spine

Will have you undressing in quick time

Don't rush this feeling; soon all of our emotions will combine

I want you to be naked by the last syllable of hello

Be prepared for this event like Last Dragon but with a Creole glow

And that's just with my sensual words and that's for sure

Place you gently in my mouth by tonguing the head

Are you sure you can handle this before we get in the bed

Some have tried but few have stayed

Best way to have me is to first be liquidly fed

Maybe then my spirits can enter you instead

Of you realizing how to be fucked within the forehead

I can start from the temple and massage you with my lips

Kissing downward to my present, thankful for my early Christmas Gift

Play around with your chest and bite on it once

I can be sensual when the moon rises or the sun is done

Taking my time to finish my role

Let's stop. So you can reach your goal

I know where it goes and it will be slow

From the tip of the head until mouth or walls shallow

Your taste makes my stomach growl

In my mouth, in my pussy, in my ass, I am on a prowl

No need for the excess to be on the towel

You see nothing to cleanup but I am wide-eyed like an owl

I am not pretending of any innocence

But I enjoy tasting your delicious specimen

Or you can rub it on me like a body cream

Visualize it over and over like a serious wet dream.

WAKE UP!!!!!!!!!!!!!

14) Our Love

Our Love is like the ocean

You are the sun

I am the sand

I can feel your soothing hands of rays

Securing me from inclement weather

When the currents try to wash me away

With the rocks, shells and debris

You are the one who beams to dry my body

Until the heat bleeds into my skin

No matter how long I lay upon you, beneath you

My tone never changes

You have shown me enlightenment beyond the mountains

Constantly surrounding me through the hikes of the terrain

Your presence replenished me, step by day

To conquer the land through the animalistic distractions

Each moment the bags becomes lighter from pain and algae

Never to be crowded but to enjoy the view with breezes

The stars greet each other

To discuss the sparkle you gave me

Undress me to the bare grain

Understanding every particle of my being

No matter, how intense the rain, you come to me in a glimpse of a rainbow

I am overwhelmed with your passion

Even though your appearance is dim to others

I see you

I feel you

All over me

This love is universal

We softly listen to the calmness of the waves

Before our departure for the night

Your subtle fire will last me until the morning

Again, Our love is the ocean

I am your sand

And

You are my sun

15). My Cat in the Hat-- Wett Wipes Edition

The sun shined bright

I was too wet but I had to play

So we sat in the house

Chilled on this cold cold wet day

I sat there with Hakim

We sat there, we two

And I said "How I wish

We had a threesome to do"

I am too wet to go out

And too cold to hang at the mall

So we sat in the house

Masturbating and staring at the wall

So all we could do was to

Sit

Sit

Sit

Sit

But we did not like it

So Hakim started licking my clit

Bump

And then

Something went bump

How that bump made us jump

We looked

Then we saw him step in on the mat

We looked

And we saw him

Sexy Chocolate Man in a Hat

And he said to us

Why do you sit there like that?

I know it is wet

And the sun is ultra-sunny

But I can make it rain inside

And have lots of good fun with all of this money...

"I know some good games we can play"

Said the Chocolate Man

"I know some tricks"

Sad the Sexy Chocolate Man in the Hat

"A lot of good tricks

I will show them to you

I am sure your boyfriend will not mind at all if I do

Then Hakim and I

Did not know what to say

Not concerned since my boyfriend was out of town for the day

But the fish said "No, No"

Make that Man go away

Tell that Chocolate Man in the Hat

You do NOT want to play

He should not be here

He should not be about

He should not be here

When your boyfriend is out

Now, Now have no fear

Have no fear, said the man

My tricks are not bad

Said the man with the long wooden hand

Why, we can have

Lots of erotic fun, if you wish

With a game that I call

Flash, flesh, and flush the fish

Put me down, said the fish

This is no fun at all

Put me down dammit said the fish

I promise, I won't tell her boyfriend at all

Have no fear, said the man

I will not let you fall

Stand by this tripod and camcorder

As I perform tricks on this ball

Lay on your back

And position just like that

Directions is not ALL I can do

Watch me spread your pussycat

Look at me

Look at me now, said the man

With strawberries and cake

Watch me lick your frosting on demand

I can hold both legs

I can hold up my fish

I can even have Hakim beg

While licking my milk on a dish

And look

I can hop up and down on this ball

But that is not all

Oh no

That is not all

Look at me

Look at me

Look at me NOW

It is fun to have fun reaching the Big O on this ball And Hakim
and I reached it together then down we fall

And our fish came down too

He fell into a pan

He said, I don't think I like this"

Oh, no I don't Chocolate Man

This is not a good game

Screamed out the fish as the grease popped but in the end everyone
ate and was eaten good to the last drop

16). Mistress

Wake up together

Recite salutation

Stranger tone heard

Calls vanished

Texts increase

Movies, restaurants, hotels

Receipts discovered

Thoughts of infidelity

Scenery evident

Daylight conserve

Moonlight freak

Bread broken

Sweat induced

Mysterious bodies

Aroma filled sheet rock

Alarm sounds

We wake up together

Smiles

Realizes

No one better

To be labeled

As

His Mistress.

17). Chair

Come here

Let me show you

Everything

I know

Sit back

As I relax

Legs on the arms

Slowly Scooting

Becoming my *Clitologist*

Opening my lips

Guess which shade of pink it is?

I want you

To undress to my moans

Fingers sliding

Amazed of the pouring juices

Don't hold back

Enough for a four course meal

Doggie bag not needed

This plate is freshly served in this chair.

18). Guess What?

No matter the day or even if I am sick

When I see you, I am going to run with my mouth open to trip on
your dick

Slowly sucking like an erotic tic

Don't readjust Oh I see that walking stick

I want you to wear this pussy out like basketball shoes

The longer you take the more this orgasm accrues

Slaughter what's yours and blast it on the 6'o clock news

Always a permanent dick aligned my walls with your tattoo

Told you before I want an imprint in this snatch

Slammed into hard like baseball with a curved catch

Bodies thrown like a wrestling match

So cum bury your face in this pear patch

Yes, position yourself you will be there for about an hour

Two fingers in my ass, I am giving you all of the power

Hold on to my legs like you are dangling from a tower

Help me release the clouds from this meteor shower

Whenever I see your meat I am completely graced

No need for your steps to be retraced

I am a cannibal and refuse to waste

All that you supply whatever the taste

I want my inside to sizzle like a soda pop

Weave not coming unglued no need for a beauty shop

Earlier I overflowed your face, no wet wipes, you needed a mop

Now it's my turn to swallow your cum like a pig eat slop.

19). My Best Friend

The call came that you were here

I knew our time together would be more than a blockbuster

Anticipating the key to unlock 416 at the Omni

Wow, this setup is priceless, speechless

And you did it for me

My eyes tell how I missed you

My mouth couldn't open

Until you lips met mine

And said, "Damn, I can't believe it's been 3 months"

Grabbed me close As if our hearts shared a beat

Looking at each other

Keeping a mental log of appearances

Bubble bath with green roses awaited me

Wine, fruit and small talk

You washed my impurities

Wrapped me and lotion every limb

Then reality hit us both

It will be an Ultimate Cumsational Fucking

Grabbed made yourself comfortable between my legs

Girl, I see you still have a pear fetish

But I love how the juices blend upon my tongue

One hand behind his head

Ankles crossed and then it happened

30 minutes later, damn I have never cum that quick

Change positions to show the workout body for this stallion ride

Up and down

Slow like a slinky

I smelled pears and pineapples in the air

Round 1 completed

Now let me taste what my garden didn't grab

From the mushroom tip to the sides

Giving that huge vein some attention

Sucking those beautiful balls one by one then two

Raising your legs above your head

My tongue slid in and out of your ass

No no, I am just beginning

My fingers begin to fight with my tongue

You are moan and moving

Whispering to stop

No,

Don't stop

Stop

I have a surprise baby

Get your reward from the back

Grabbing my dreads

Kissing my neck

Speaking dirty, sensually, erotically, poetically

Okay, now put it in my ass I will open up just for you BOOM...

I swear the entrance sucked him in like a sinkhole

Pounding Thrusting Gyrating

Until nothing for me to grab

But myself

Then the spirits congratulated us again

Just like in previous encounters

We have once again tackled something only read

Once Upon a Time

But the love and passion is real

Shower Sleep

Then we return to our day to day lives

I love fucking my Best Friend.

20) The Other End

It began at 7:05 am

Musical ringtone

Greeting exchanged

Said, "Just do what you are told and nothing else"

Hands on nipples

Seductively squeeze

Allow other hand

Trace the outline of your body

SShhh, not a word only soft moans

Introduce it to your clit

Allow them to free between

Close your eyes

Imagine

Fingers are my tongue

Paint your ship

Salivating brush

Stroking the outer and inner

Harmoniously

Graceful slid

Juices formed while applauding

Swaying like flowers

Internal drip

Fruit-flavored dew

Don't speed

Slowly

Wider

Legs

Wider

Freshness of your fruit

Exposed

Covered fingers

Nectar between them

Word filled gyration

Cryful moans

Just cum with my thoughts

21). Purpose

I saw as it began

As a peach fuzz

You shape it

Asymmetrically

You were pulling

Stretching

Like it was your dick

Poetically

It became

Longer than your chin

Let me tell you its purpose

To rest my lip

Upon your lips

While your hairs

Tickles my ass

See my juices saturate

Your mountain covered palace

For this ultimate queen's throne

Strokes of your tongue

Played on my clit

Professional Bass Player

My pussy squirt in your nose

Breathing

In my essence

Freshness

See, your purpose

My juices embedded like a nest in the tree waiting for the birth

The more I pretend to be comfortable

I just change angles for additional enjoyment

When I am finish

Your pores will be *Creologically* drenched with my love for you

Naw, it is the love of you

Just realized wet wipes isn't enough to hold my juices

I need your beard

22). On the First Ring

Close your eyes

Let yourself go

Drift away to my commands

Kissing on your earlobes

Hands sliding up your shirt

Caressing the insides on the way down

Left to right nipples getting harder

Unbuttoning your pants

I put my foot in the middle to allow one leg free

Pushing you on the bed

Gradually sliding your legs up

Kissing the head, shaft then nut sack

Giving each undivided attention

Feeling my spit down the crack of your ass

My tongue searching for nuts in a snicker bar

Warm mouth gradually welcomes your dick

Damn I missed you

Up and down

Side to side

Inch by inch

Up and down

Inch by inch

I can feel it reaching for my tonsils

Throbbing

Pulsating

Shaking of your dick

Ready to explode

Massage your balls like fuzzy pecans before the crack

Pussy juiced finger in your ass

Come here

Don't run from me

In and out

Out and in

Mouth dripping for your manhood

Sucking your dick like a Watermelon Big Head Blow Pop

Damn, you are scrumptious

Precum on my tongue

You made me wait

Pull my locs

Fuck my sweet mouth

You know you want me to have it

Harder

Faster

Harder

Faster

My fingertips dig into your thighs

This shit feels so good

Ride my mouth for life

Feed me

Feel it

Slowly

Sliding

Into my hole of secrets

Come on

Feed me

Pimp my tongue

Slave my throat

Let me drink your soul

Ummmm, have good nap baby

23). Passion Provider

He wants to comfort her

Beyond the comforter

I loved his aroma filled persistence

For her affection to be offered for a lifetime

Never thought it was really for me

You see, our eyes never met

Until months before my sun

Crept upon a sensual dialogue

Only the moon could understand

Again, never thought it could be for me

His words played between my ears

Like a classical saxophone serenade

Soothing an untamed and ignored beast

Caressing my inner and unrecognized beauty

Awakened by the smiles upon the morning dew

Centipedes walking through cerebral vibrations

That only a musician can anticipate the rhythm

Finding the ingredients of my hula hoop

To dance with only the syllables of nothing

Until that day his presence touched me

The fluttering of his tongue from my ankles

Reversing my power struggle within the sheets

Saturated from imagination of what is to come

My body deepened within his skin

Reaching for more and less simultaneously

I felt my mouth moisten for his entrance

A one way ticket into my wonderland

With each article of clothing falls from the trees

Allowing the leaves to expose its strength

Beyond his eyes in the autumn season

His hands turned me like a spinning top

Engaging in electric cosmic energy

The world stopped existing with each stroke

Breathing, breathing, breathing for a release

Damn, he is experiencing this with me

My mind broken like a jigsaw puzzle

But my body is swinging on an unforeseen twister

Accomplishing the incense filled walls of our thoughts

We can't turn back from this experience

Enjoying the crashing through danger signs of lovemaking

He conquered my pear flavored entrance

Slowly, charismatically and methodically

Planets dancing wildly, humming an erotic chorus

Encouraging us for a finale unimaginable

To the ordinary steps of mere mortals

The collision of our buildings

Being constantly constructed

Each time he kissed my neck

Thoughts, words and actions made it unlock

Whispering in my ear

That he loves and in love with me through the storms of Zeus.

As the moans increase through the recipe of poetry and lust

Our own spirits witnessed from the heavens

How the rain poured upon us

As he unwrapped this beautiful and lonely box

Not understanding what is to come from Pandora

Sensual is what he gave me until my skin

Combine with his for the ultimate Creole Southern Comfort Bar

Uncontrollable slow grinding intense motions

I can't stop this world wind of penetration

For this hunger is greater than any scientists can imagine for him

He climbed upon me with such ease after our rebirth

Like a caterpillar nibbling upon a delicious leaf

Caressing my breast, kissing me down the sides

Of the body seen by a few but as if he is my sculptor

And I will forever be his masterpiece of passion.

24). Left side

As my body begin to snuggle

Within this cold satin sheets and pillows

I slowly entered to lie on my left side

With hands warmly pressed between my thighs

Thinking about the moments of breath upon my neck

And the smoothness of those fingers around my waist

Guiding the rhythm of 10 tips of pleasure

Waiting the glimpse of juices to flow

You whispered in my right ear

Gladly allowing my right leg

To be lifeless over yours

So there is no doubt of the mission to begin.

25). One Aisle Night Stand

I went to gather new items for dinner

Wishing for something to get my attention

As I search for the ingredients

Our hands met

Casual apology but he didn't let go

Maybe someday that meal will be with me, said he

Slowly moved away, smiled, continued my shopping

This red bone bow-legged caught my glance with those hazel eyes

Damn

Gave a casual hello

Then a dark chocolate dread gave me chills

His tone was as strong as his eyes

"Call me for an experience", whispered my lips

Wow, sexiness is definitely in here tonight.

So our encounter earlier met again

From the produce to the home ware

Guess I will see how good his tongue game is

His name is...well it's not necessary

Approached me and stated

I want to slow grind your mind but fuck you from behind

For your ass is as plump as a case of plums

He slid my pants down

Opened a magnum from his cart

Slid it like silk over my leg

Yeah it was like that

Tilted my body, left leg in his hands

I thought I was top shelf

The way I was holding to those racks

Moans filled the store

Items being thrown

Until my knees were on pillows and my head on a comforter

We fucked for 30 minutes like dogs in the Sahara Heat

The earth shook with our eruption

Cleaned up and gave me his, "Overseas Delight"

Damn, what the hell was that?

Trying to get my composure

Wobbled to the electronics to check out something smooth

The clerk said, "I can make you cum in 10 by letting you fuck my face"

Immediately thought, this is the best grocery shopping trip ever.

He slid between my legs like a shoe salesman

Ensuring his tongue was a perfect fit

He slurped me like he hadn't eaten in weeks

But he was amateur and aim to please with perfection

7 minutes later

Out of nowhere that red bone appeared

Handed his card in the middle of my leg shaking orgasm

Read…

Videographer

Thank you for participating in this One Aisle Night Stand.

26). Tonight

Tonight will be extraordinary one

While engaging in penetration and cunnilingus while swinging

The force behind the motion will be transferred

From the ceiling to the hinges of the doorway

I want to be sucked like a crawfish

With all of my juices seasoned for you

From my head to my tail is enjoyable

Better than anything natural, drinking me at your leisure

The stroke of our pendulum is gratifying

From the heat escaping my loins

Confined from running or dehydration

Reaching the utmost outer body explosion

Positioning me like an acrobat

Moving limbs in adventurous ways

Having feet touching ears while tasting me

Allowing hail to fall from the sum and quenching our thirst

Body displaying goose bumps as I look into your eyes

Mumbling the syllables "DO WHAT YOU WANT'

Secured with momentarily bondage

Your hands wrapped around my neck

Firmly pressing to intense the pleasure

Our forever safe word is "Pears"

As my moans begin to increase

Finding my jewel with every inch of your tongue

Damn, the word escapes me to describe the excitement of our love session

Imaging the stars dancing through my eyelids

As the squeezing becomes sensual but mind boggling

Of the way you beat this pussy like a piñata

For you to gather an ultimate treat

Pounding, slurping and thumping of your tongue on me

Will give you a lifetime of sweetness to enjoy

Tonight will be an extraordinary one

While engaging in mere foreplay while swinging

The force behind all of these motions

From the ceiling to the hinges of the doorway

27). Offer

Several months passed without being opened

Wider than Niagara Falls

Offering a canoe for excitements

Yes, I am saturated

Head to toe of memories of our last visit

Contemplating your tips

Across my nips for seesaw licks

Yes, this playground engraved from your presence

I curse your government

Creating love lines to deepen within my skin

Yes, I love you

Love you from your mind fucks

Body sucks

And the way my soul bucks

At the mentioning of your name

I convulse to the verb penetrating in my pear

In and out

Up and down as your lip and tongue dance sticks through my plasma

I am gone

Gone from the shivering of my legs

Grabbed within your clutches

Choke me with sensual confinement of abduction

Exploring me like lost mail within the seven seas

Scavenger hunt this pussy

Dominance and submission

Searching through my walls for buried treasure

Measuring the lengths of my juices

Yes, it pours for blocks

Warm icing covering your mouth as my cake

Damn, I am offering

Myself

To do wild things

Strange things

Just fucking things with you

Unchain my desires with sensual fires of passion

No, passion is not needed just pure lust

Lust the fuck out of me

Let me suck you whole

Allow my mouth to change colors like strobe light popsicles

Until it is gone

Yes, gone from your dick

So, would you accept my offer?

28). Quickie

Slide your fingers across my velvet tip

Explore my rivers and valleys

From the top of my mountains

To the bottom of the seas

Enter me

1 finger

Umm

2 fingers

Ummm

3 fingers

Until the moisture covers your hand

Deeper

Harder

Slower

Faster

Open me like a can of pineapples

Place your tongue between me

Lick around my desires

Slurp the juices you created

Finger-paint this pussay

Creating famous portraits

Spreading wider

Circular movements

I am your bad girl

Legs forming V's and M's

Body making lower and uppercase S

Your head game causes an orgasm to shoot from my mouth

As the hungriness of your tongue eats down south

I squirm like an earth worm

As you bless your food with your grace

Without missing a stroke

Facelift performs emotions and expressions

Causes hallucination and slurred speech

When you partake on my clit

I can handle this kind of quickie.

29). Mount Up

This is the time for you to understand

That I want to discover your uncultivated land

After this adventure, I will become half of your pituitary gland

So allow my hands to play like a baby grand

Let me slide one leg out of your pants and shoe

Have you ever had a mental rendezvous?

Imagining you are my chocolate fondue

Let's see what designs it can develop into

Allow my skin to crawl upon you like a spider

Slowly attacking within this seductive insider

Grab the pillow for my tongue will now be the guider

Of arousal with a mouthful of sweet cider

Gradually slurp each ab that you formed

Conservative to freak is transformed

In the room changing from sunny to stormed

Your birthday suit is worn as your uniform

To the top of your body from whence the tingling begin

Knocking down your insides like the wall of berlin

From your ears, to your face, down to your chin

For any weapon you have, I am forever your firing pin

Hips are moving and legs are wider

Time to prepare for comfort as your horseback rider

Mount Up!!!!

30). Midnight Step

Hidden within the shadows of an edible sacrifice

Graceful eyes unnoticed among the unprepared longing for my prey

I creep upon you as you played in the field

Admiring this meat which allow excessive hunger before the act

I hesitate

The smell of your masculinity sends my stride rapidly

Still unrecognized

Brisk breeze of your fragrance

I am severely excited and I approach slow and sensual from behind

My paws around your neck

The bite was quick and untraceable to the naked eye

Stunned from this doomed adventure as your soul is crying to be mine

I whisper, "You didn't know that I was watching"?

Purring becoming heavy as you are trying to break free from my grasp

Pounce on top to feel all of your body heat

Loins vibrate to the flow of your blood

Spine numb from the attack as this is a passionate kill of the heart

Quivering how our bodies are in sync

Warmness of your meat upon my tongue

Struggling

Squeezing

Enjoying life as you knew it being released

So

Let go

Please stop fighting

You have been captured by a midnight step.

31). Detox

He came into the room

Noticed the wetness of my box

Like sweating through a sauna

Crackhead binges

Methhead scratches

Weedhead munches

Hungry for his dick to swell

My well with pulsating steel

Rod to enter and exit my holes

I want him so bad until my clit throbs

Leg shaking, juices brewing

He performs triangular strokes

Screaming to taste me upon his lips to my lips

Ready to explode

Moaning cries within the neighbor's walls

Through exasperating groans

Reaching for clouds and moon for help

Me to release my dreams

Turned reality through suffocating thrusting

So my cum can drip his name in cursive

Manuscript your dick within Shakespearean thoughts

Sipping his scrumptious load in a Communion Cup

Fill my insides like hot apple filled Krispy Kreme on a wintry day

I need a Detox

He puts my clit in a cast

Second set of lips in a sling

Given stitches from your Boom…Boom….Bang

Afterwards begging to be soaked in Epson Salt

Body glazed after our sexual christening

I am thirsty for his hot thermal

White chocolate covers my tongue and mouth

Smoothly drinking like a Kellogg Protein Shake

Creation performed on my glands

I want his cum to splash my face

Like the wind of a rollercoaster ride

Slowly smearing on my lips like my favorite gloss

Damn, he tastes so fucking good

Anticipating for my morsels to melt in his mouth

Addictively my pelvis thrust

Begging to unlock my candy crush

Promiscuous as I sit and wait

For him to access a free pass for the next ride

I love how he snorts me like goodie powder

While I constantly lick my lips as I inject him like marmalade

Tic

Toc

Time for Detox

Carl Danford

Name Carl Patrick Dunford.
Age 51 living in Germany.
Originally from Nottingham England.
Studied catering at Clarendon catering
collage Nottingham .
Worked at various hotels before joining
the Royal Air Force as cook.
Served for Six years ending service
In Germany in 1989.
Started writing in my teens.
Only been writing erotic since six years.

1) Secret love

The secret I keep is so real.

I can never tell you,

how I feel.

Should I listen to my heart,

should I listen to my head.

My head aches for you,

my heart, bleeds for you,

I yearn for you.

This secret is one,

that can never be told,

wrote about, or sold.

This secret is about you,

where ever you are,

in my heart, you are

never far.

I will take this secret,

to the grave, think of all

the pain I will save.

And when the time is right,

I just might see you up above,

when I will tell you,

you were my secret love.

2) Star Gazing

Went in to the garden tonight

a million stars

twinkling on high.

Thoughts a long way from home

my mind began to roam.

The brightest two stars

they were us

sealing our love.

Many miles away

guiding the way.

There I was alone

sitting on my own.

The person I needed next to me

was like the thoughts in my head

a long way from home.

And like the stars out of reach.

3) To Share

Legs open wide

skirt pushed up to thigh

panties nowhere to be seen

your pussy a dream.

Shaven not a hair in sight

adds to my delight.

Your lips moist

you really have no choice.

My fingers travel high

slowly teasing

gently easing

Spreading

opening wide

allowing my tongue inside.

Now tasting your inner delights

I hold your thighs tight.

Probing deeper

moving faster

feeling your dam burst

quenching my thirst.

I love to share and you want me to

so I move my mouth to kiss you.

4) Tease.

Slow you like to tease

unzipping slowly

your skirt below your knees.

Your top still on

this is half the fun.

Panties sexy and with a bow

this gets me hard

I think you know.

Little by little I see more

will it be your top

or your panties

that kiss the floor.

Will I see your breasts

and nipples erect

or pussy so hairy

and wet.

I am watching and waiting

to see what is next

to see when your

bare to see your pussy

and your hair.

To dream of what I see

to wish you were part of me.

Slowly you tease

for you I would do

anything to please.

5) Winter romance.

Snow laying on the ground

everything so white and clean

a winter dream.

My baby and I walking under the

night sky crunching sounds

as we walk

holding each other close

no need to talk.

She has never seen snow before

looks on in awe.

Strange it seems

to some people snow only

exists in dreams.

While the people who see it

at winter time often moan

about how cold .

Winter can be romantic with two

alone with each other

wrapped up warm

to hold off the storm .

Just like my baby who has not seen snow

winter and all that it brings

is full of romantic things.

6) Heaven sent

You like to tease You like to please

I love it when you are on your knees.

Your fingers so long and slim

nails painted red

only you know how

to touch

how I like it so much.

You take me in your hand

wrap your fingers around

nails teasing the skin

I am ready to begin.

You pull down

the head on view

shiny just for you .

Your lips open wide

taking me inside

I can feel your tongue

as my body reacts

now there will be

no holding back.

Your mouth a trap

for my cock

only you have the key to unlock.

Deeper you take me inside

your eyes open wide.

As your mouth works its wonder

I can feel a rumble

my body starts to shake

a human quake.

Erupting till I am spent

Your mouth is heaven sent.

7) Destiny

I took you to Paris

I took you to Rome

We never left our home.

Our imagination was allowed

to run

free how it should be.

We went for walks along the beach

looked at the moon above

swore our love.

The world was ours to do

what we will

no tears did

we spill.

Just us too many miles apart

together as one in our heart.

Writing sweet nothings

only we could see

happy in our own company.

Not for one moment believing

we would never be

this was our destiny.

We planned the future

and told of things we would do

when I finally met you.

Of simple things places to go

swearing I love you so.

That dream I still believe

will come true

my only fear is I am loosing you.

Our time got less it really

put us to the test.

Please let me take

you to Paris and Rome

again just like way back then.

Let us walk along the shore

look at the moon above

and swear our love.

knowing this is meant to be

it is our destiny.

8) Office Vamp

She was a tease

she knew how to please

with a flash of thigh

she caught my eye.

Raising her dress higher

all I could do was admire her.

No panties did she wear

her pussy had golden hair

did she do this for a dare.

She was normally shy

always avoiding my eye

Now she was bending over

allowing me to see.

Her breasts not in a bra

the best I had seen by far.

Caught a peek my knees

went weak.

She whispered in my ear

with her hot sultry breath

if I would like more

I nodded my head.

Our office was empty

other workers on a

break

she was undoing my buttons

she could not wait.

In to the store room she led

the old table a make do bed.

With foreplay in full swing

she begged me to put him in.

This once shy woman

was a devil in disguise

she had the look of lust

in her eyes.

She gripped me tight

till the time was right

and when that time came

it was the end of our game.

The woman so shy

who could not look me in the eye

went back to her desk

not a word said.

9) Foreplay.

Finding out what you like fingers exploring

Oral mouth to mouth kisses sweet

Reactions I see telling me it is right

Erect I am rising

Playful no disguising

Letting our fingers roam

Arousing sounds echo around the room

You whisper in my ear the message is very clear

10) Self love

Men and women may deny

Ask them outright and they go all shy

Something often seen as taboo

Too bad we already knew

Under the covers or in the shower

Randy couples do it in pairs

Baby oil nothing spared

Any way you can discoverers new

Toys whatever you like

Every ones does it am I right?

11) My Angel My Devil

Eyes that talk

lips with a smile

to melt your heart

this is only the start.

A heart that beats

with the rhythm of love

so good to be part of.

A voice from above

an angel my love.

Eyes twinkling

almost winking

lips begging

to be kissed

more of this.

The heart now thumping

almost jumping

Pushing out her chest

exposing her breasts.

Her voice now a command

letting me know

I am her man.

Sexier than before

almost a drawl.

No longer from above

my devil

my love.

12) The Wall.

Picture the scene

the one where you

have always wanted to be.

Pushed up against a wall

panties pulled to knees.

Your top ripped off

you said you like it rough

breasts set free

your nipples hard for me.

My hand spreading your legs

like you always said.

Kissing your neck

my mouth nipping your skin

you all hot within.

Nipples in my mouth

fingers working below

your breathing heavier

with every stroke.

Parting lips feeling you wet

fingers pushing in

from your mouth a whim.

Undoing my jeans

I set my man free

standing proud

for his entry .

With an almighty push

I feel your pussy gush

pinning you against the wall

fucking you as you wish

my mouth on your lips

sweet sensual kiss.

Spinning you around

face against brick

now its your asses turn for my prick.

One fantasy that today

was reality .

Another thing to cross of the list

the list of sexual bliss.

13) Your Man and Master

Sitting there legs open wide

panties by your side.

Your lover your man

sends his commands.

Spit on your finger

rub your clit

punish the bitch.

With your other hand

pinch your breast

tweak your nipple

till it hurts.

Feel the pain turn in to

sexual joy

now grab your toy.

Tease pussy lips

slide it in fuck your self

thinking of him.

Your man:

He likes to hear how wet you are

it turns him on makes him hard

loves to know which bra.

Imagining you playing legs spread

sends him over the edge.

He tells you when to come

you listen to him.

The pressure hard to bear

your pussy about to explode

still he tells you no.

14) Pantie feast

She was waiting on the bed

not naked but legs spread.

Told me yesterday of a way

to please.

How she would like to be teased.

Today that fantasy was about to

come true.

She was wearing panties of blue.

I got between her thighs saw the look

in her eyes.

Started kissing her legs tongue teasing

doing its best.

Reaching her crotch I could sense she

was hot.

My mouth licking and kissing

her pussy pulsating .

Tugging and nipping with my teeth

a sensual feast.

She wanted to cum

with her panties on

just me and my tongue.

I could see the blue turning darker

Smell her aroma

hear her breathing

her moaning.

As my mouth began to eat

Her vagina began to weep.

She was coming in gushes

I did not want to rush this.

The taste of lace

Mingled with her nectar

Ask me I will tell you

nothing better.

Soaked panties and torn

bitten in lust

another crossed off the list.

15) Visual mind.

Imagination setting you free

taking you to places you

long to be.

A visual mind the key

for experiences

that would other wise

not be.

Letting you kiss and caresses

fondle and tease

while typing with the keys.

Setting the atmosphere for the night

wanting everything to be all right.

Words on the screen seem on fire

describing sexual desire.

Kissing imaginary breast

tummy and below

the words just flow.

Words appear telling you

feel the same

enjoying our game.

Hearts beating blood pumping

only the beginning.
The screen now blue

as we follow through.

Visual in our minds

and so intense

no longer pretense.

The feelings now real

emotions too

longing to be with you.

Both reaching the point

of no return

the screen now all wet

imagination is the game

as we both came.

16) Do You Scream My Name

Lying on your bed

curtains drawn light low

your favorite music

reminds you of not so long ago.

Fully clothed but for how long

listening to your favorite song.

As the lyrics take on

a meaning you understand

thinking of your man.

Your body heat now rising

you take off your clothing.

Top and skirt are the first

you gracefully throw to the floor.

Lying in panties and bra

your hands wonder over

your breasts.

Fingers in panties

feeling your wetness

Now slowly teasing your clit

as thoughts of me

run in your head.

Pushing your bra aside

one hand playing with nipple

the other hand below

leaves your clit and

opening you lips.

Your fingers you guide

to your moistness inside.

17) Bath Time

Relaxing dreaming

surrounded by foam

bathing alone.

Hot water tingling skin

feeling warm with in

ready to begin.

A body massage with soap

setting the mood

giving hope.

Foam applied to legs

razor sharp removing hair

rinsing almost there.

Sitting on the edge

applying between legs.

Taking care sensitive lips.

No longer a landing strip

rinsing admiring the view

the new you.

Stepping out hair dripping wet

water droplets on your breasts.

Toweling yourself dry

you think of your guy.

Again the sound of wet

echoes from your thighs

accompanied by a sigh.

Not from the water in the

tub this time it's while

you rub.

18) Blue.

She walked in to the store

bras on show and so much more.

Looking for that special pair

with her lover to share.

The curtains drawn she started

to undress jeans and panties

around her legs.

Removing her bra she admired

her figure. She could still

poke out some one's eyes

when her nipples did arise.

Her tummy not quite flat

her lover was ok with that.

Her vagina with a landing

strip

above her hidden clit.

The new bra she had on

her breasts full in this one.

New panties to match color blue

a sensual hue.

Sexy and frilly lace

she could not wait

to see his face.

She took out her phone

took some pics

with the message

how bad do you

want this.

19) Exploration

Exploring new exploring you

Getting to know your mind

the secrets you hide.

Looking in to your eyes

the answers hoping to find.

Kissing your lips holding you close

promising not to let go.

Feeling your beating heart

only the start.

Whispering soft in your ear

the message clear.

Our night to share

Love and lust

not able to resist

wanting more of this.

Bodies entwined as one

breathing each other's air

hands massaging there.

Body parts erect

moist between legs

your full breasts.

Together we fit

in unison we move.

Only a matter of time

when we have reached

our journeys end.

May be later to

start again.

20) Body Evidence

Your pictures were only the start

how you found your way

into my heart.

Getting to know the real

you took it's time

now forever on my mind.

I tried to deny my feelings for you

only now

do I know they are true.

If that is good is not

for me to decide

I only know

I cannot disguise.

A figure and curves

that leave me wanting more

play heavy on my mind.

These images I take to bed

playing over as I touch my self

wishing it was you instead.

Telling you what is happening below

not wanting to let go.

Sometimes I see you

in your bra

and panties too.

Other times I see the naked you.

The images I wish they were real

so I could touch and feel.

Love to explore

and may be more.

Let our inhibitions free

making love softly.

Seeing your smile

waiting for the sign

knowing we will cum

in time.

Your legs and tummy quiver

cheeks a rosy red

evidence of our love

trickles down

your leg.

21) Chocolate Treat

A sticky treat just for two

chocolate sauce and cream

a lovely goo.

Blind folded led to the bed

while you prepare

I wait there.

The time has come for

me to remove the fold.

To see you

covered in chocolate

legs spread.

A mixture of that and cream

any man's dream.

With someone who has

a sweet tooth like I

this is sexual paradise.

Chocolate sauce on every part

where do I start.

From the top

working down

first your breasts

a delight

nipples protruding

a lovely sight.

Tummy is next

my mouth so full

never getting

enough of you.

My favorite part

I will savior

this mixture

now has a new flavor.

The sauce and cream

with your own between

mouth to lips

teasing chocolate coated clit.

This was a special treat

tomorrow it's your turn

to eat.

22) Cyber Lover

She was sitting across from me

thanks to the cam I could see.

All that she had to offer

if only she was here

and not on the screen.

I would love to run my hands

down her body

kiss those lips .

Too feel to touch

to smell her perfume.

To hold those breasts

in my hand

tease the nipples with my tongue.

She was probably thinking the same

in our cyber-sex game.

How she would love to

hold my cock

to tease my balls.

With her finger tips

circle the tip

awaiting her lips.

She was playing with her pussy

I was playing with my cock.

I could see she was wet

she could see I was hard.

I heard her breathing louder

fingers going in deeper.

The other hand on her breast.

Teasing the nipple with that look

that is only for me.

I began stroking my cock faster

my hands cupping my balls

I was giving it my all.

My cyber lover

was moving faster too

her pussy glistening

like morning dew.

We both know when the time

is right after all we are here every night.

My cock is ready to release

she is saying cum baby cum

with one last stroke

I ejaculate my sperm

hitting the screen.

In real life it was where

her breasts would have been.

My lover arches her hips

as her pussy opens wide

her juices trickle down

the inside of her thigh.

We both light a cigarette

looking pleased.

Tomorrow night

she wants me to fuck her

on her knees.

23) His Queen

Seeing old haunts

the memories remain

time can't take away the pain.

The walks across the park

in the woods hand in hand

I could have been your man.

The museum and the car park

where we had our fun not caring.

Only eyes for each other middle

age lovers.

That seems so long ago last week

The memories clear.

I felt as if you were there.

Now in contact once again

this man will not give up

to follow his dream.

Making you one day

his Queen.

24) Internet Whore

Far away in contact on the net

having never met.

Seen you once on cam

Wished I was your man.

It was my words that attracted you

if only you knew.

My words I would love to put

in action giving you satisfaction.

Making love soft and slow

turning up the crescendo.

Making you beg your pussy wet.

Sometimes fingers may be a fist

you are on my bucket list.

Pussy whipping biting and spitting.

Your master I say

you dare not disobey.

Fulfilling our fantasies no taboo

me fucking you.

Telling me what I love to hear

feeling you here.

Stroking my self-thinking of you

all the things I want to do.

Our sex would set the room on fire

so hot is our desire.

Our bodies scratched and bruised

fuck how I want my muse.

25) Jewel

A treasure a jewel

hidden from view

belonging to you.

Not a diamond

more a pearl

your little girl.

She can rise

when aroused

or hide when not

technique and

know how counts

a lot.

She will take you

to places new

places you never knew.

Send signals through

body and mind

start a chain reaction

one ending

in satisfaction.

Alone or with some one

with finger or partners

tongue.

She will thank you

when she comes.

26) Master and Lover

I am in charge of you

I say and you do.

No matter where

I do not care.

It pleases my twisted fantasy

gets me excited

knowing you like it.

You describe to me

how it feels to touch

yourself and play.

I love it this way.

To touch and explore

your soft pink folds

may be hear you moan.

I tell you to rub faster

you do I am your master.

Now we play this little game

telling me your ready

I say stop.

Knowing the affect

pussy dripping wet.

Throbbing begging

pleading to let you play.

Wait darling it is better this way.

What seems hours later

in reality minutes

I tell you to finish

happy to obey.

No more words for

a while.

Then appears "dripping down

my thigh"

Panties soaking

a throbbing body shaking.

As your master and lover

new worlds we will discover.

27) Role Play

You said you like it rough,

from soft you have had enough

gives you a thrill,

you want to be my whore.

You want me to,

push you against the wall,

rip off your top,

lift your skirt high.

The sound of material being ripped,

the pounding of my dick,

your pussy now so wet,

I'm not finished yet, you're screaming, for more,

how I hate you whore.

Yes this is really fun,

I've been fucking you, so long,

I'm ready to cum.

Take me in your mouth, lick me dry,

please don't cry, maybe I got carried away,

you said you wanted rough,

for today it's enough.

28) Sweet

Strip now

do as I say

want to see

how horny you

are today.

Take off your bra

throw to the floor.

Offer your breasts to me

nipples hard and free.

Let me take them in my hand

rubbing and kissing

nipples flicking.

Slide your panties

down your legs

beckon me between

your knees.

Slowly tease.

My hand touching yours

ready to explore.

Fingers in deep

juices begin to seep.

One word comes to mind

that word is sweet.

29) We fuck we make love

We screw we fuck

make love.

Cannot get you out

of my head.

wish you were in my bed.

You love your neck kissed

bitten or nipped.

Your breasts cupped in my hands

massaging the nipple

watching them rise.

I look up in your eyes.

As my nipple I take in my mouth

my hand wanders south.

Meandering down your tummy

to your honey.

Touching your outer lips

rubbing over your clit.

Hearing you moan calling my name

over again.

If in the mood for rough

the kissing nipples I bite

my two fingers I push in

knowing your tight you do

not fight.

Sensual we can be to

whispering I love you.

Holding you close

breathing your air

fingers running through

your hair.

Exploring your body with care

though not the first there.

Giving you pleasure

teasing your treasure.

Taking us to places new

fucking loving you.

30) Voyeur

Let me watch you play

Please today.

I will watch but you

will not see

I will be the voyeur

hidden away

enjoying the show.

Rubbing my self

nice and slow.

Act one you lay naked

on your bed

legs wide open spread.

Act two your fingers

against your lips

with saliva coated

you tease your nips.

Act three is the part

that I like most

your other hand

down below.

Teasing and knowing

what it does to me

you play with your pussy.

Act four a moan comes

from your lips

you are touching

your clit.

As I watch my hand

undoes my zip

jeans fall around my hips.

My hand around my man

working as fast as

I can.

Act five you really

come alive.

fingers massaging breasts

other hand on pussy lips

you start to arch your hips.

Act six the second to last

you put a dildo in your ass.

Fingers in pussy deep

Moist and shiny

all I can say is oh blimey .

The finale is not far away

rubbing faster you say

cum baby cum for me

cum on the count of three.

As if for encore and on time

you let your juices flow

I pull once more

before I blow.

Darling that was

some show.

31) Undressing

Sitting opposite her

mentally undressing.

Taking off her clothes

one by one not finishing

until done.

She wore a blouse

underneath a bra

May be black or blue

I wished I knew.

From the shape of her chest

I could picture her full breasts,

nipples large not quite hard.

Her tummy with its own curves

leading to below.

Where not any one is allowed to go.

I would like to say she was shaven

that is the impression I got

if not she was still hot.

I bet she wore panties of lace

may be plain white.

Or blue to match her bra

maybe commando.

My mind now in over drive

my trousers began to rise.

It was then she caught my eye.

I thought she would get up and go.

No.

She gave me a show.

Her bra was blue panties too

guess what she was shaven too.

Waiting room.

Sitting opposite

I can only stare

she crosses her legs

all is bare.

Its late in the afternoon

both in a waiting room.

She must see the effect on me

shuffling in my seat

trying to hide my bulge inside.

Her mouth opens fingers

raised to her lips

moments later

covered with spit.

She looks at me with

a sensual stare

places her fingers there.

To the spot which makes

her hot makes her melt.

Where her pink flesh

will be stretched.

Carried away in a world

of her own I hear her moan.

Suddenly everything is still

We both had our thrill.

A voice on the intercom

she is next.

She raises to leave

her seat wet.

Freknardo

Flenardo Taylor's passion for writing poetry is used as a way to tap into his imaginative side of life. He recognizes that it was never a talent but a gift from the Most High, whom he considers the greatest Spitter to ever walk the planet. He believes it was Jesus' kiss that ignited poetry within his soul.

He writes without limits; there isn't a title or subject that he cannot touch. He lives in an alter ego state of mind where Freknardo is a Ferocious Warrior and Flenardo is the Humble Lamb that keeps everything balanced.

Freknardo favorite quote is "I write like a virgin but I perform like a whore".

Flenardo is currently living in Alabama (United States) and he can be contacted at http://freknardo.com/

1) Words Upon Your Chest

Have you ever had a poet to lay words upon your chest?

A poet that can spit words to make you want to get undressed

 Words that cause you to become possessed and obsessed that you want to take them home so you could molest the words you didn't have time to digest

 I spit words like they are my Sunday Best and if you confess, I promise to bless you with my best

 This is only a test but I have all the answers. Just let me tap into your mind as your erotic dancer

 Dance these verbs and pronouns into your mind until you mentally breakdown and drown in this rush of poetic tides that will flush out your insides

 As these words slip and slide into your brain like a runaway train with no brakes. Leaving you with pleasure and aches at the same time with just a small dose from a poetic mind

2) Stimulated Scratch

I love your nails, every detail; the color, length, power and the strength.

I would love to taste your fingers like they have been dip in Heaven sauce.

Spread them apart like Angel's wings and dive in between them over and over again.

I would gently kiss them one by one until your heart rise like the morning sun.

Passionate pecks to stimulate your nerves that will make you whirl your curves.

When I sip your tips, you will move your hips.

I'll take my shirt off so you can scratch my back.

Scratch deep into my skin like you are digging for gold.

If I had an Orgasmic itch, then I want your fingers to make love to my soul.

3) Just My Imagination

When I was a kid I would imagine me traveling to distance lands. Holding hands with a picturesque woman that would obey my every command.

We would play in the sand and swim nude in the ocean. I love when she would come outta the water dripping wet. Her hair is down to her back and I want to blow on her body like a clarinet.

I would rub her body down with lotion and whenever we make love, it would be in slow motion. Drinking up each other's emotions like love potions.

She never complains about a thing because in my mind I am a King and I own everything. I know all her thoughts before they come out of her soul. She loves to take over and I enjoy when a woman takes control.

 I want to squeeze and never let go. I would treat her like a free throw, the game is on the line and I want to celebrate by sending chills down her spine. Kissing her like juices off a watermelon rind.

We would count the stars at night until we fall asleep. Then all of a sudden I would wake up into reality. Not even the real world can take this woman away from me. I'll just pick up a pen and recreate my vision with poetry.

4) Frozen in Time

She sits and ruminates over life trials and happiness. She knows that life comes with joy and sadness. She thinks so deep that time will freeze, the sun will pause, and the birds will stop flying. She likes to think into another dimension where only love can take you there. A place where time last forever. A place where peace and sunshine can make love together.

This is her new heaven on earth. A place where a woman is treated like a Queen and worship for what she is worth. She sits and stares into another galaxies and imagine a man that can pick her up off the swing. Play with the strands of her hair and say I love you my beautiful Queen. I'm your shiny knight. The darkness will never absorb my light. My royal status is so deep that they will need telescopic sight just to view the small things I can do with delight.

For starter sit back down and let me get on my knees. You choose the color and I'll paint your toes, massage your elbows, back, shoulder, neck, and legs. Today we can make life breathe again. Now we need some music, I snap my fingers and the birds start to sing.

We will go back to the days of old, where Kings serves their women even in the pouring rain. Tell me about your day as I continue to wash, scratch, and pull the strands of your hair. I will listen and enjoy your conversation with no thoughts of fornication. I will listen to what makes you special, what make your heart beat, and watch you smile when you think of me. I would touch your chin and glide it down toward the sand. Say closed your eyes and you will hear the wind blow and it will say open. You will open your eyes and all you will see is my footprint but you will exhale because I left my scent.

5) Moonlight Lover

You can keep the sunrise; I want it so dark that I can barely see your eyes

That's where our passion lies, between the cool breeze and the midnight skies

I just want to take you, make love to you until you evaporate and disappear

All I want to hold is your scent in my hands

I can still hear your moans like the owl that sing throughout the night

You are the beautiful woman that I hear in the moonlight

By the water I'm ready to take a big splash

Dived in head first, ready to quench my thirst

By the moonlight, I'll take my pen and erase your pain

I'll take the paper and ball away your emotions

I'll wash away your worries with every kiss

Never leaving the soul of the woman I miss

This is love making at moonlight without even lifting a hand

You say you are hot, and then my body is the shade

If you are thirsty, then my tongue is the fountain

Hungry then my mind is your meal

I'm the truth and I'm real

Superman can fly, but he's not the man of steel

I'm the moonlight lover

There's no need for sheets and covers

Under the stars and by the water is where I will conquer your soul

Won't stop fulfilling your destiny until I gain all control

6) Cowgirl Ride

I want a woman to ride me like a rushing tide, drowning my soul every time she grinds my inside. I need her to sit on me and twist in all directions. I want her to ride me while she makes faces in the mirrors so I can see all of her expressions through her reflections. I am not even looking for a hard ride, something smooth, sort of like a glide. She would squeeze her muscle every time she reaches the tip. Then oozes her body back down and slowly kiss me on my lips. She would moan my name real slow as I feel on her nipples while she twerk it back some more.

I am rock hard; I feel like I can shoot to the moon, she say hold on Daddy, I don't want you to cum anytime soon. She bucks me until you can see the ripples in my abs shake. I love this ride and I should have buckle up if I knew I was going to be in an earthquake. She takes her time to blow my mind. She slowly turns around and rides me backwards. I see that this woman is trying to turn me into a coward. I'll be sensitive tonight, no need to be the Freak, sometimes it's alright when a man retreat.

I can see her ass goes up and down, she holding on to my ankles while she is breaking it down. She starts to do the tootsie roll on my soul. If she does the electric slide, I swear I will cry on the inside. She rises back up like the morning sun and whisper Daddy, I am still having fun but I'll ride harder if you promise to cum. She gets up on her toes and starts to jump. Damn I am really enjoying looking at her rump. She grabs her own hair and buck back and side to side. I close my eyes and I can feel the energy I am about to release. I shoot a load and fell right to sleep. I need a cowgirl with a killa pussy to come and murder me.

7) Come & Eat

Come and Eat baby, I got the special cream that you can smear your face in. I know it's your birthday so I am ready for the party to begin. Freak just eat, I need you mouth, tongue, and nose in all 3 of my holes. My cake is your wish so just blow. Blow out the back doe, then kick in the front, I want you to eat, moan and grunt. I told her that I was ready to eat her cake, layer by layer without stopping till it's all gone. I want to eat her cake like a beast, call me King Kong. I blew out the candles and stick two inside of her vagina. Then lick the cream off. She moans and say eat some more. So I rip off her clothes but told her to leave on the hat. I started to chew on the cake and then spread the rest on her body.

Just looking at her naked and sticky made me so hungry. So I just buried my face in between her legs and she clamps her thighs around my head. She told me to lick deep, hard, and fast. Then when I finish, turn her over so I can suck her ass. I did as I was told, so I lick her clit in every space and even lifted up the fold. I didn't even miss a spot because she was screaming that I was making her hot. She rolls over and I place my tongue over her butt cheeks. She exhale and said blow me. So I blew cool air inside of her space. I place my thumb inside to open her up. It's my birthday but I am about to give her a beautiful tongue fuck. Once again, I did as I was commanded. I dug in that ass like I was trapped in quicksand. I made her cum with the licks and the tongue sticks, and then she got up and wipes the cream on my dick. She lace it up

real well and said I am about to blow on you like hell. So she
started to jack me off just for a minute or too. Told me to close my
eyes and enjoy the show. She hums on my balls and then glided
her tongue on my shaft. This is the best birthday present I have
enjoyed in a long time.

She said I am going to keep sucking until you start bucking. She
said she wanted to leave me dry and satisfied. I knew exactly what
to do. So I wrap my fingers in her curly hair and pump her tonsils.
She couldn't talk because her mouth was full. She took both hands
and started to twists and turns my dick as she kept swallowing my
head. I loved her mouth and she knew how to fuck up my head. I
kept pumping these strokes into her soul. I told her I was about to
cum but that made her lose more control. She wouldn't stop until I
release my wish into her mouth and out it came. Damn I need a
birthday like this every day.

8). Giving Head and Swallowing- Green Eggs and Ham Remix

I am Freknardo

I am Freknardo

Freknardo I am

That Freknardo-I-am

That Freknardo-I-am!

I do not like

that Freknardo-I-am

Do you like

giving head and swallowing

I do not like swallowing,

Freknardo-I-am.

I do not like

giving head and swallowing.

Would you like giving head and swallowing

Here or there?

I would not like giving head and swallowing

here or there.

I would not like giving head and swallowing

anywhere.

I do not like

giving head and swallowing.

I do not like swallowing,

Freknardo-I-am

Would you like giving head

outside?

Would you like giving head

In my new ride?

I do not like giving head and swallowing

outside.

I do not like giving head and swallowing

In a new ride.

I do not like giving head or swallowing

here or there.

I do not like giving head or swallowing

anywhere.

I do not like giving head and swallowing.

I do not like swallowing, Freknardo-I-am.

Would you give head and swallow

in a box?

Would you give head and swallow

If I promise to stop?

Not in a box.

Not if you stop.

Not outside.

Not in a new ride.

I would not give head or swallow here or there.

I would not give head or swallow anywhere.

I would not give head and swallow.

I do not like swallowing, Freknardo-I-am.

Would you? Could you?

in a bed?

swallow! Give head!

Here is my head.

I would not,

could not,

in a bed

You may like swallowing.

You will see.

You may like swallowing

in a tree?

I would not, could not in a tree.

Not in a car! You let me be.

I do not like giving head and swallowing outside.

I do not like swallowing in a new ride

I do not like swallowing in a box

I do not like swallowing if you promise to stop

I do not like giving head or swallowing here or there.

I do not like swallowing anywhere.

I do not like giving head and swallowing.

I do not like swallowing, Freknardo-I-am.

A train! A train!

A train! A train!

Could you, would you

Swallow on a train?

Not on a train! Not in a tree!

Not in a car! Freknardo! Let me be!

I would not, could not, in a box.

I could not, would not, if you promise to stop.

I will not give head and swallow outside

I will not give head and swallow in a new ride.

I will not give head and swallow here or there.

I will not give head and swallow anywhere.

I do not like swallowing, Freknardo-I-am.

Say!

In the dark?

Here in the dark!

Would you, could you, in the dark?

I would not, could not,

in the dark.

Would you, could you,

in the rain?

I would not, could not, in the rain.

Not in the dark. Not on a train,

Not in a car, Not in a tree.

I do not like swallowing, Freknardo, you see.

Not outside. Not in a new ride.

Not in a box. Not if you promise to stop.

I will not give head and swallow here or there.

I do not like swallowing anywhere!

You do not like

giving head and swallowing?

I do not

like swallowing,

Freknardo-I-am.

Could you, would you,

On a boat?

I would not,

could not.

On a boat!

Would you, could you,

If I ease it down your throat?

I could not, would not, on a boat.

I will not, will not, if you ease it down my throat.

I will not give head and swallow in the rain.

I will not give head and swallow on a train.

Not in the dark! Not in a tree!

Not in a car! You let me be!

I do not like swallowing in a box.

I do not like swallowing if you promise to stop.

I will not swallow outside.

I do not like swallowing in a new ride.

I do not like giving head and swallowing here or there.

I do not like giving head and swallowing ANYWHERE!

I do not like

giving head

and swallowing!

I do not like swallowing,

Freknardo-I-am.

You do not like swallowing.

SO you say.

Try swallowing! Try swallowing!

ANd you may.

Try swallowing and you may I say.

Freknardo!

If you will let me be,

I will try swallowing.

You will see.

Say!

I like giving head and swallowing!

I do!! I like swallowing, Freknardo-I-am!

And I would give head and swallow in a boat!

And I would give head and swallow if you ease it down my throat...

And I will give head and swallow in the rain.

And in the dark. And on a train.

And in a car. And in a tree.

Giving head and swallowing is so good so good you see!

So I will give head and swallow in a box.

And I will give head and swallow if you promise not to stop.

And I will swallow outside.

And I will swallow in a new ride.

And I will give head and swallow here and there.

Say! I will give head and swallow ANHYWHERE!

I do so like

giving head and swallowing!

Thank you!

Thank you,

Freknardo-I-am

9) Ode to Lyrical Gymnast

My tongue has gone through rigorous training to prepare for the Lyrical Gymnast. I have revamped my oral techniques so I can please you with tingles from your head, down to your feet. As you change the hair color of your head. I too want to tongue fuck you until your face change colors as I serve you this head. I want to suck and pull on your clit until your blue eyes turn brown. The Gymnast likes to be flipped around and I'm not fucking around when I go down. So flush me with your juices. I refuse to drown until I suck the sounds outta your moans and bite into your pussy like a snow cone.

My neck game is serious and ready to flex, time for sex, leave you confuse like the butterfly effect. I want to slurp on your pearls until your toes curls. Then slowly stop and lick straight up your chest so I can dive into your breasts. Kissing them soft, gentle, and just right until I take a small bite. Licking them with the right tempo, because I love freaking my Poetic Monroe nice and slow. Then you have my permission to push my face back down because I don't want to come up until you cum out. That's the shit that I'm about and when you cum on this tongue and hum your favorite climax song. I am going to penetrate this dick in you real quick as you yell Oh shit.

Pin your legs back, way back and attack your pussy until it goes flat. Pounding your ass with the force of an earthquake, the bed I am trying to break because I refuse to slow down even if my dick came with an emergency brake. As you cum again and the juices are flowing down my soul. I'll politely ask you ride my pole. You jump on it with no hesitation, and I grab the back of your ass so I can shoot this fiyah in your gut, real cremation. So as you ride, I am arching my back so we can meet up for this explosive fuck. You grinding, I am winding as the sweat from our heat is melting the sheets. I just don't release seeds; I sic them on your ass like Pitbulls and Rottweilers. Go ahead get face down and ass up, because this shit is about to get wilder. As I slap that ass while I eat that ass, then lick my fingers because your taste is too sweet of a memory to let any of it go to waste.

10). Love Thy Self

I have no problem pleasuring myself and I refuse to be ashamed. I have power in my hands to call out my own name.

 I close my eyes and stroke intimate fantasies of wet panties and perfume. When I want to be romantic, I'll light candles and bring my own sexual ambience into the room.

 I like to touch myself to music because they say it soothe the savage beast. Tempos I increase and decrease until I am ready to release.

 Yes I do moan when I am in my zone. I play my instrument likes it's a trombone and I'll thrust inner power from my hipbone.

 If I really get into it, then I'll make the bed rock. Throw my knees up as I begin to buck. This nut will come and when it does. Its shoots up my chest, once again these hands are bless regardless of the mess.

11). Vision is Clear

I want to dive into your mind so I can play with your thoughts tonight. If I am going to please you then I need to know everything that makes you feel alright. I want to scroll through your nerves and use this tongue to swerve off course so I can split your body in half like a nasty divorce. Then I would use these lips to stitch and patch your body with one single lick from this mouth piece. I am about to serve you harder than a prisoner on work release when I release this oral pleasure that will disturb the peace. Your neighbors will automatically call the police. I am on a mission to become your love slave. I want to wave this tongue in your cave until you burst your tidal ways that will send shock waves hard enough to make the dead rise outta their graves.

I am serving you tonight.

I am going to take my time with this sixty-nine and if I miss anything. I'll go back in time just to lick anything that I left behind because your future orgasm would run through walls and up your spine. I know you like taking pictures so I have mentally taken a snap shot of all of your spots that I shall eat up when you open your legs up.

I am in no rush at all so whatever position you call. I shall not run but crawl into your abdominal wall that will make you shake your hips like you are in a dance hall. Your orgasm will tear down your soul like the Berlin wall. I am ready to please you because your picture is my inspiration. I am thinking about your walls clenching my face to cut off my circulation. I will never need ventilation because I am your slave and I will eat anything to reach my Emancipation.

12). Full Service

She said I need a tune up- a real maintenance man, one that can serve and fill me up as many times as he can. She said I need a full service, are you qualified to diagnosis the problem and fix me. A smile came to my face and I said well, I never been to school to learn my trade. I can look at the problem and mentally fix it in my head before I pop the hood. She said that's all talk, I need actions. I said you better read the sign first then I'll guarantee you satisfaction. My service includes sucking toes, licking ass holes, and I'll even suck your elbows and kiss any other place your man refuses to go. I have no problem getting on my knees; I'll even have knee pads because

I am a pro at working beneath. I like to get under the hood, flat on my back, trying to look for any leaks or loose springs. Baby I can fix everything.

I'll toot your horn, clean your windows but you gotta let me take it for a spin. She said hop on in. I jump in the driver seat, and ram the gas. She caught whiplash because of the way I took off so fast. I was switching lanes, driving like I had road rage, cussing and fussing but I was willing to do whatever to make sure her service was complete. She was like slow down, you are scaring the shit out of me. I watch as I hit the dips and every pothole in the road. She said you must like it rough. I said I drive like a bat out of hell. I beat that car all down the highway. When I pull back into the garage, her hair was all over her face. Make up was dripping off her chin. I laugh and told her that my service can leave you with a smile on your face. She laughs and said I'll recommend your shop to more of my friends. I said go ahead. I gave her a lollipop to suck on as she walks out the door. I'll tune up whatever is broken down; best believe I got the best service in town.

13). Tango

I dip her on the dance floor; inhale her passion as the music consumes our mind.

She drops the rose as my presence send chills down her spine.

Her hair swags back like a cool breeze coming in.

My eyes are focus on hers while I caress her smooth skin.

I am giving her the dance of a lifetime.

When the music stops, her heart will drop.

I speak no words just rhythm

If she came in here with blues, she will leave with happiness

I slowly glided her back up and lifted her above my head.

Let her ease back into me, I want her to grind me

Not nasty but freaky.

She rocks her hips and she slowly invites me to kiss her lips.

I do the tango with my tongue.

If it isn't the dance, it must be the kiss that has her sprung.

14). Suga Shak

There is something special when a black woman smile, memories
that soak into your heart and make you want to change your
lifestyle. Yes you have the perfect name. I am feeling your name
so deep in my mind that is causing my toes to crack. Let me taste
your Sugar because they say suga means a beautiful, hot, young
and sexy female. A word that is found only in the South. Leaving
my words lost in my throat so I can't speak when I open my
mouth. Did I tell you that you are beautiful this morning and my
heat is pumping and thumping inside of my chest? Suga also
means damn!! And you need to be charge with a crime for killing
that dress. I am honored if you just ignore me and let me just look
from a distance and admire your legacy.

I love your heels and the way that belt is wrap around your waist,
make me want to ask for a taste. See I don't want to taste your
body; I rather taste your mind. I want to taste your memories and
your dreams. I want to swim in your history and work hard till I
earn a spot on your dream team. Is it possible I can go back in time
and replace the man that took you out on your first date? Hold your
hand, and show you a good time, and have you back home before
nine. Then we can hop back on the phone and have conversation
until the sun rise.

Your name is sugar and did you know in the old days they used to
chew on sugarcane raw to extract their sweetness and best believe
if I had the chance I will bite on you all so I can taste a piece of
your happiness. So I guess I would ask God to transform me into
an ant because I would build an empire for my Queen. You just sit
back and let me cater to you. Sugar is used to sweeting life when it

is sour and I will enjoy your sugar poured over my soul for hours. So when I look at this picture, I overlook what the world see, I just want to create a beautiful memory. Well tasting your mind and beauty was a pleasure to my soul and if no one else tell you that you are beautiful, then I am telling you that you have confidence on cruise control. I would love to stare at you until I have an asthma attack; damn I always lose my mind when I stare at the beauty of the Sugar Shak.

15). Ascento Sensual (Dom Chula and Freknardo)

It's been a long time since the last time I got down on my knees N pleased him

A very long time since I unbuckled his belt, unzipped his pants N pulled them

Along with his boxers down to his ankles

I wanna lick the tip of his dick with my tongue…

Give his head wet sloppy kisses while rubbing his balls with my hands….

Slide his cock in N out of my mouth while I French kiss his shaft

AND…..

I'm still not using my hands…

Feed me Ur meat daddy…

Let my esophagus meet your head…make it tingle in the back of my tonsils

Allow Ur semen to become seamen swimming down my throat because we know that…

Milk does a body good N baby you taste like creamy coconut milk …Ur not salty at all

Damn! Your mouth taste like heaven, I'll never sin again

Because I love the way my balls are bouncing on your chin.

I am ready to explode, don't worry this Freak packs an automatic reload.

Your mouth must have a secret code, so I am tapping this dick down your throat like a Morse code.

See I love feeding you my meat but I need your clit between my teeth.

Do you want to serve me on top or beneath? Open Sesame!

Just trying to see will your walls open up for me so I can dig the treasure within thee.

I have been dying to choke off your chocha till I swallow my last breath.

If you got that killer pussy, then I am ready to taste death.

Please gyrate your hips in my mouth like you are doing the Rumba

And I will have you dripping sweat like you were teaching Zumba

I am going to suck out your emotion and eat away the fragrance of your scent.

When I am done tasting you, my country grammar will develop into a Spanish accent.

Worship on Ur knees as you lick my clit

Baby let me feed you. Give you this juice I been saving just for you.

Are you thirsty?

Well open your mouth

AND

Take big gulps from this water fountain between these thighs

U

Love

Writing

Ur

Name

On

Let me ride your face backwards as I deep throat your magic stick

Abracadabra it rises

With every stroke of my hands sliding up N down your dark chocolate cone

It's gonna melt in my mouth N leak onto my breasts….

Go ahead rub it in like lotion N watch my nipples stand at attention

Spread my legs wide as you slide ur thickness between these slits of pink flesh

Let me lead you to the treasure in this tunnel.

Choke my chocha

Wrap ur hands around my neck

Make me lose my breath

I'm moaning loud

Passion filled thrusts is what you inject me with

Let my fragrance linger on ur fingers as you make ur country
grammar mix with this Dominican mami…….

Having me screaming out "aye papi…I'm fixing to cum"

DomChula

I love seen you relinquish your juice and I am eager to swallow,
best believe my dick is soon to follow.

Follow its way into your chambers where I can have you singing
musical notes every time I baptize your soul with these powerful
strokes

I need you on your stomach, because I want to talk in your ear as I
ride that pussy like my name was Paul Revere.

There will be no Red coats coming but my dick will be gunning
and running in you like an athlete.

Tonight you shall feel every inch of me because you are my MVP.
Most Valuable Pussy

I plan on leading us both to victory. If you promise not to faint, I
promise to deposit all of my sperm inside of your bank

Every time you back up that ass, I'll slap that ass because I want it rough and fast.

I'll finger your clit while my dick continues to split your ass like a banana.

I am on a mission to break your ass like the levees in Louisiana

Let me mount your Stallion N ride you till the sun rises

Temperature continues to rise like the waters in New Orleans

There's a hurricane surfacing from inside my walls

Keep packing your meat in my gut and splash paint all over these walls

I wanna see what your name looks like in white

I'm gonna rise your dick like my life depends on it

Make your toes curl N ur eyes roll in the back of your head

Backwards cowgirl so you can slap my ass as it bounces up&down on ur hard erection

This is perfection the way we make this look easy as we work up a sweat…..

Touching…teasing…..pleasing

This

Is

Not

A

Race

He paces himself to make sure he cums last

Making sure I unload at least 7 shots while he's stroking me

Go ahead and get ur victory……Cum for me

16). Blindfold (Freknardo and Teaspoon De Peculiar Treasure)

I have no choice but to treat you this way. This is the real meaning of erotic foreplay. I tied your hands to the chair so you can't stop me when I place my tongue there. I blindfolded you so you can't see how many times you will cum, but you will feel every time you leak, drip, and run. I want to fuck you a little rough tonight. I am going to pull that red dress up and your suck the pulse out of your clit. You going to love the way I eat your shit. First I am going to suck on your toes, then lace this tongue up your legs. I know you moaning but I ain't quite ready to give you head. I am doing figure 8's on your thighs as you are begging me to stop. I reach your pussy and I watch how you throw your legs into my face with a tight headlock. I love when you buck. It makes my tongue act up. I finger you with one, and then two, then I lick my fingers to sample you.

I won't be here long, just a few more sucks and your orgasm will come on home. You squirt and I can feel the sting on my neck. Now I will break a little sweat. I grab your legs and throw them on my shoulders. I am a rough muthafucker, never a weak soldier. I start to drill you like I am digging for oil. You know my shit shoots to the sky so I can't wait till my dick reach your G-spot and say hi. I am tonguing you in the mouth and fucking you hard and deep. You let go of my tongue and scream please don't stop. I am slamming into that pussy like a dunk contest. I am cutting this pussy up from all directions that you are thinking that north is now west. You begin to shake and squirt on my dick with so much force that it knocks me back a few feet. As I watch your pussy drip, I do what I love best and begin to sip and eat.

Teased & taunted. Beyond what I wanted. Oh yeah I want it. Begging pleading needing. Body screaming jerking. Convulsions twisted twitching your sudden movements outer workings. First dessert. Then dinner. Delighted with Splendor. I have no choice but to surrender. Being controlled by The soft whisper of a baritone / tenor. Under complete & total submission. No intermissions or my permission. Him having his every which AH way with no intension of stopping.

Breathless I breathe and heave in between jaw dropping. Kisses given deeply mouth coated. Tongue to tongue then slightly touch the back of my throat hushing whatever I noted and grabbed the back of my neck's nape. He gently drapes over me softly like a windblown cape my legs become undone ajar then agate. Whaaaat the FUCK! is he doing to me? As I shake. Between the pleasures of pain my mind can't differentiate. He hesitates watching me contemplate. He mentally fucks as well as physically stimulates. I assume as he consumes me from the middle of my ass cheeks. He kisses me again as I try to speak.

 Trying to Look down no avail Blindfolded tight without a peek. Feeling Fingers walking, fingers fucking, clit touching,clit gushing. Teasing me more intensely by his penis against my pussy brushing, slightly never rushing. I scream out "Fuck me now before I go insane." From The bulge of the veins & nerves as it grows into a large curve. I came again as he was on the verge of entering into my welcoming opening. So well-endowed I focus in. He takes his time as he begins. Flexing my legs out so My Ankles are at my chin. Palms my rear end lifting me up from the chair Whispering so calm "Fucking go insane" in my ear.

His strokes were precise to witness. I didn't want to come in an instant. Breaking down my resistance. I felt the stretch of my vaginal walls tighten and loosen with the down pour of wetness. Soaking his stoking. He was striking bringing the thunder like a Viking. The fine dining was to his liking. He ate like a king! and ate damn everything!

17). Goldi Locs (Freknardo and Ms Creoleness)

Once upon a time there was woman name Goldilocks who would
walk through the forest butt naked. Playing with her pussy and
wiping the juices on trees and leaves. She came up to a house and
knock but no one answered, she walks right in. She was hungry for
some dick so she notices 2 dildos and one pussy pocket. She licks
the pussy and said not bad but I tasted better. She sucks the first
dildo and said it could be thicker. She sucks the last dildo and said
it could be longer. So she went to the chair, found a Kandi Kisses
Massager, and begins to rub it against her clit. She felt the
vibrating sounds as she arch her back and threw her legs higher to
release the nut. After the wet and juicy nut, she was ready to go to
sleep. She looks at all the beds and tried the first but it just
wouldn't do. She looks at the second one and said nah, not so.
Then she found the third one, said perfect, and went to sleep.

Awakened naked, with my pussy being eaten lips smacking and
legs opened to receive all of him. He slurps the juices from my
thighs, fingers this honeypot and puts two fingers in my mouth. He
performs tongue flips on my clit like an imaginary spoon twirled in
my bowl. I can feel the porridge escaping my walls. He said,
"Open the fuck up wider". His grizzly tone excited me so I
greedily accepted his request as he slid his chocolate monster
slowly into cock drain, dick taste like deep dark chocolate. He
stirred hard as the spit rolled down my chin. I can only imagine the

sweetness of his nougat on my palate. I can feel the eruption creeping and then another voice said, "Let me get some of that"

Bitch you are in my house slurping on my Papa dick. I am about to grab you by your golden locs so you can slop on this pussy. Since you like to eat porridge, you will love the way Mama Bear taste. I am about to fuck your face until your jaw bones crack. You keep on riding that dick and don't stop you little hoe. Ain't shit free in my house but nuts and thrusts. I begin to finger my clit and yeah it's hairy as hell. I am a bear bitch. I don't shave. I wipe my juices down the side of your cheek. Then spread my legs over Papa bear face so you can eat. I grab you by the head and slap your face. Eat you filthy slut! Eat bitch. I am going to cum all in your mouth. You are sleeping in my bed like Dru Hill. Swallow this meal.

I thought I would fight but your smell is so sweet. I will eat your pussy drier than Nevada. Grabs my locs bitch as my tongue make your reach for stars never created. Fuck me harder, jab this pussy Papa Bear, you know you want my hole. Spread your fucking cheeks Mama Bear and howl my motherfucking name. Ride my face from here to Amsterdam. I am hungry for you as your man get high off of me. Drip jelly and jam from your ass and I will eat that too. Goldi is a true freak ain't too much I won't do to you. My pussy and mouth stay hungry, fill my throat Bitch and empty my pussy Nigga. Put your hairy legs on my shoulder and stop running from me. Ohh I see your ass ain't talking shit now. So let's see how Papa Bear fuck you while I eat his out with these Gummis.

Bitch I want to fuck you in your asshole but first Mama Bear needs her thirst. Go put that strap on so we all can ride along. Mama bear get on your knees, Goldilocks go ahead, slaughter that pussy, and hit it deep. I am about to fuck you in your ass like Bad Santa, you won't be able to shit for a week. We are a three way train. You are going to remember breaking into our house. Now I am about to cave in your back door, you little whore. Take this dick. I stroke it hard, spit on your back, and slap your ass cheeks. Now keep fucking Mama Bear until she begs you to stop. Our screams equal the sounds the Giant made when he fell from the beanstalk. Our breaths are harder than the Wolf and the pigs. I am about to dig in your ass until I end up in China. I am about to leave my balls inside of your anal walls. Mama Bear you better not cum before me. This bitch must work for her food. Make her earn every piece.

Fuck me Papa Bear; go deeper into my honey cave. Mama Bear fucking you is incredible because your pussy so tight. Squirm, moan and bite the curtains off the windows. All the animals would know about my crime. Break in this asshole while I enter into her pot. You can't punish me, I love fucking threesome, both of your ass will scream my name. Mama Bear moving her body like a Bee to hive video, bitch you can't hold that nut give me my shit. Papa Bear thrusting his pelvic until I felt his long dick in my damn knees, he grabbed me by my locks screamed "GOLDI" and exploded his hot porridge on my back. That shit felt like a geyser in the Never land until I came with the chorus of birds. Mama Bear came and screamed like she was given birth, I tried to break her tailbone as she cried "LOCS". Mama Bear fell on her face; Papa Bear fell on his back. I snatched off my strap on and threw it on the table. Every time you mother fucking bears eat, you will taste me until then I got a date with Red Robin Hood. Holla!!!!

Yes baby, we still have the floor and this Freak is still ready to explore. You have been begging for this dick, the tongue and a whole lot more. You are the first woman outta thirteen and I am going to invade your spot. I am going to leave my tongue so deep inside of you that it might just rot. See baby, you was talking noise and I love how you want me to spread your legs and taste your cream. You see I bought some whip cream and strawberries for this scene. Yes lie on the floor and lean back. I am about to suck the pulse out of your pussy cat. Leave you flat-line every time I curve this monster from the tip of your clit and wipe your behind. Yes you w ere right, I am a freak, and I love to eat, now do me a favor, and pump your ass into me.

Two things are going to happen while we are on the floor, either you are going to get a splinter in your ass, or catch whip lash while this tongue whip and lash. I love a woman that grabs my head and punish me while I feast; I automatically turn into a wild beast. Now pump that pussy into my mouth, I want to catch your juices on the tip of my tongue. I will swallow your seeds. Consider me Johnny Appleseed, I am here to cater to your every needs. Yes grind your hips into my nose, let me smell your scent and inhale your soul. Yes baby, faster, harder, give it to me raw and uncut until you bust that nut, I want to feel you release the energy from your gut. Give me what I need, I want to digest every last one of your organs if need be, now bust that nut for Big Daddy.

Yes I know you are cumming and the thirst is so damn mind blowing. Now roll over because this cock is hard as a rock and I know your body is hot. Hell yeah this dick is about to taste the sweetness of your sweet spot. I am pulling your hair with one hand and slapping your ass with the other one. I am hitting your pussy so deep, that I can see the ripples in your ass riding against me. Yes baby take this dick, take all of my shit. Faster, Harder, Stronger, you begging me to ease up and slowdown in your spot. Nah baby I am about to beat this pussy until your stomach turns inside out. You are yelling Freak, I am cumming and I wanted to cum with you so I release my load. Then I jump outta the pussy, grab the whip cream and strawberries and suck out everything I just shot in your spot. I taste your juice mixed with my protein. Water is flowing from your eyes, your hair is a mess, and your nose is dripping snot but I will do it all over again if you let me eat your sweet spot.

Another Poetic Pussy talking about how she going to take my money. Since you say you can savory the flavor. Then how bout you just let me explode in your mouth. I promised this impact will be worse than the trade towers, when I deliver this shower. Yes I am wrong, but you just prepare to take this ding dong. I know your name is Passion Fruit but tonight, I am not in the mood for fucking, but as for you, get to sucking. This is how it goes down. I will stand and you will get on your knees. I'll be nice so you can get on the bed, if you say please. Good girl. You open your mouth and I lower my rod like I am fishing and you took the bait. Nasty cheap skate.

I love my freaks that just can't wait. I am just getting head tonight, so suck, lick, blow, but don't fucking bite. I started to grind my dick all through your mouth, and your mouth feels good. I will call it the tunnel of love. I grab a fist full of your hair and started to speed up the strokes, you licking good, daymn good but I ain't got all night. So as I pull your hair, you should see the way my ass is pumping this dick. You said slow down, but nah, take it. I push you down and make your head turn sideways, Insert this dick again and I am pumping so harder than before. As you open your mouth and I am imagining that your mouth is your pussy and I am doing it just right.

I am pumping and I grab your head to match the speed of my dick, Yeah daddy going to shoot a deep load in your mouth tonight. You are going to drink this nut tonight. Yes baby, aww yes! Drink this dick. I know you are wishing I will hurry up but don't fuck up my mood. I am stroking and I can feel the nut on the tip of my dick. You ready for this nut, you scream yes Daddy, feed me. Then I pull out and shoot my cream all over your face. Then I grab the fruit and place one in your mouth. I said suck on that. Get dress and get the fuck out.

Gag Ball, I been ripping holes in the other ladies soul. Tonight I just want to take it easy with you. You are the third victim for tonight and the tenth this week. I know I started out as a poet but I am just possess, just hush and get undress. Why must you wear the gag ball? Well I don't feel like hearing, oh God, I love this dick, and I love you, Oh shit. I just want to go to bed feeling good and lit. Just put the ball in your mouth and let me suck on your inner thighs, swirling this tongue in all the right spots. Planting kisses all down your legs. Yes baby, you are special, you deserve this. I kiss down your legs and start to suck on your toes, one by one, and I am licking between every space and I love the way they taste. Then I roll back up and look you in your eyes. Your mouth is gag and I love the peace, then I roll you on top of me. Let you ride my face and wash my mouth with your cum. Yes baby ride these lips. After a long day of a whack school teacher and a nympho, I deserve to relax tonight with a woman that loves Freknardo.

As you continue to ride, can you feel the way my lips are licking your tip, do me a favor, spin backward and ride my face from the back. You spin and I love eating you out right. You start to increase the speed, I suck the same tempo, and best believe it will take all 13 of yawl pussies to stop Freknardo. I love the action, the booty smacking, the lips waxing. You grab your titties and twerk that ass till you cum down my throat, I am so nasty I spit it back up and blow it out my nose. Then you jump right on my dick, bouncing that ass hard and strong, the music is just right. Marvin Gaye, let's get it on. Yes we are getting it on and you bend down and grab my ankles and ride this dick harder. Hell yeah it's going to be a good night. You ride and cum and cum again. I take the gag off and you say. Daddy may I, and starts to suck my dick till I explode and you keep the juice in your mouth. I reach up and kiss you and drink my own shit, why? Because I am a freak of another kind. I kiss you on your forehead. Shower and got dress. You ask when I'll see you again. I smile and said only time will tell but if you ever get tired of that boring family. Come and fuck with me. She smiles and said fuck them, your dick is all the family I need. I said that's my girl, and I strip out of my clothes and dove right back into her soul.

You know getting in the tub is an excellent plan and you blowing me underwater might make me lose all control. You are so beautiful and your words are digging into my mind. I refused to freak you tonight but I will make love to you. After you come up to breathe let me get on my knees and show you why I have a third lung. I will be under the water so long that you will think I have an extra tongue. Just close your eyes and let me massage your worries away. Let me eat the stress away. Let me blow your problem down and let me do that over, and over, and over again. You need this, just relax, and if it feels good. Go ahead and sink your claws into my back. Yes baby! Scratch me up real good, leave, marks all over me. If eating your pussy underwater is a crime, then I am forever guilty. I love how the bubbles and your juices are foaming inside of my mouth. I hear you calling my name; you want me to rock the boat. I come up out the water and slowly insert my manhood into your motherhood. Shit feels good and I am biting on your ear with every stroke. Yes you like that, because your sensual spot is so wet and full of life. I refused to knock it hard, but nice and slow. You know like Tina Turner and Proud Mary, My sex is not scary but some like it rough but with you, just nice and slow. After an hour of giving you the slow stroke and you are still cumming for the tenth time. I pull out and start to lick your breast; I refused to cum tonight because this night is all about you. I want my tongue to be like a confession and I pray your pussy can keep it a secret.

My My My, How quick have the mighty falling. Who's your Daddy? Who pussy is this? When I unzip my pants get on your knees and prepare to kiss. What was the last word you said right before I fuck your damn brains into the bed? I am truly sorry for the way your nose hit the headboard when I was ripping that shit from the back. Yeah I heard you bragging how you are a bully in the bedroom. How you can make men submit. I must admit your pussy felt like it had a mouth of its own down there. It's a damn shame that I am already dress, and your lifeless body is just lying there. I love a woman that enjoys the rough stuff. I love a woman that says a man never gives her enough. Yeah you started off hard in the paint now you just another freak screaming OH MY GOD! I am beginning to think I am turning sinners into saints. You said you will swallow me dry. Well explain to your friends how I reloaded in your mouth then pull out and shot some in your eye. Fucking bully my ass. See my dick never get tired, I just love to stop and eat so when you riding me, I am really trying to suck out your ovaries, kidneys, and going for you heartbeat.

So ride it cowgirl, ride this mouth, I want to drink, sip, lick and taste your juice. I will gargle that shit. Spit it in the air. Catch it then swallow and then tell your ass to bring it. Now ride this face you nasty cowgirl. Wanna be a bully; make me beg to stop eating this pussy. I promised I won't stop. So you bounce hard trying to prove me wrong. I'm still begging for more. You are sweating and screaming, damn nigga give up but I keep smiling and licking while slapping you on your butt. Finally you get tired and just roll over. I jump up with extra energy because I have stolen all of yours. I pick you up and throw your ass on the wall, fucking you with strokes and slapping you upside your head. While I grind this dick in you, I start pinching your titties and biting on your neck. You want to be a bully, well take this dick. Fight me muthafucker. Then I pick you up and slam you on the bed, you are moaning and groaning. I started off doggy style with these hard and fast strokes. You deserve to have it rough, take this dick. Then I pull your legs and pull them down, pull out my dick, and then I went back in. I push your legs together and went back in your pussy hard and strong.

I am jack rabbiting this pussy, I love the way I am fucking you hard. You are breathing hard telling me to stop, nah keep going, you are so damn confused and lost. I don't give a fuck about your feeling this is rough fucking and I am the Boss. You scream Freak as you cum on my dick. I love it, and I keep pounding, pounding, and pounding. Slapping that ass, over and over again until it turns red. You are begging me to stop. I don't give a fuck so I pound and slap that ass all over again. I pull out and shoot cum down the back to your ass crack. Spelling Fuck you bully with my semen. You lay there. Refusing to move. I shower and got dress. Your lifeless body just looks fuckup. You is pathetic I will never tap out.

I truly love your name so after tonight. I rather you love me than hate. You know I am going to fuck you so good that you will trade on your sisterhood. Damn I love that line! Say it with me. You are going to fuck me so good, that I am going to trade on my sisterhood. Yes you are learning. I am going to make you an example of how good this dick, tongue, and body is rocking. You did a beautiful job bobbing my balls. Your name is too sweet. I just refused to let you suck my dick so as I play in your hair. You just continue on playing tug of war with my sac.

Yes baby you are doing a wonderful job. I know you want to speak but your mouth is full. Just let out a sweet drool and I will know you are playing by my rules. I'll do the talking you just keep on sucking. Your sisters already know you are a traitor, Umm Hmm, say it again for daddy. Umm Hmm. You know when I started this mission everyone told me I was committing suicide but I lived on the wild side and I am the biggest freak worldwide. You are the sixth victim of the pussy patrol, the rest of them are in ICU with their pussy swollen. Well except for that freak I left in the bathtub that almost drowned. Silly ass clown. Anyway, your times of sucking my balls are over.

I know you don't like been tied up but you look so cute. Suck on this fruit; relax, while I finger your cat. I part your legs open and finger your tip, then lick and twist. You want me to do it again. No need to answer, I know you do. I love eating pussy, but I think I want to slurp on your tank. What! No man ever did that and they call you Juicy Dezire. Well I'll take you there. Get on your knees and I will slurp the tank likes it's a Georgia peach and my lips are like a leech that will bite and hold on tight. You are moaning Freak, please undo the chains. I replied I am not here to torture you but to nurture you. You need this. I am a good guy; I love your name so much that I want you to fall in love with me.

Yes I slowly dip this tongue in and out of your pussy slow and steady. You love it and you squirt on my tongue. I come up and throw your legs behind your head and buck that pussy for a few strokes. Then I ease back down and suck your clit some mo. Licking your sweet sticky stuff and loving it. Doing it just a little faster this time. Then I insert this dick for some deep strokes, pumping and thrusting in and out, out, and in. Then I stop and lick some more. You say stop and just fuck me but I just want to pleasure the woman that betrayed her family. You saying you can't turn on your sisters but my dick will make you murder your own parents. I laugh and say now you are learning. Then I just dived in that pussy deep. Pick you up by the waist. Force fed your ass to me until you came and said please don't hurt the rest or the ladies.

Yes you are a poetic slut and I like that. I'll be your poetic maintenance man. I tell you what; I will play your little game. I'll even let you call me nasty names and even act like you running thangs. I like the high heels, the stocking and the maid outfit. Now jump on this tongue and do a fucking split. Like Too Short, baby I love this freaky shit. I agree with you that missionary is so dead. You need to let me suck on your brain that creamy crotch. Now this might be explosive, ok you can handcuff me and why you at it go ahead and blind fold me too. Do me a favor, put the ice in my mouth and ride my fucking face.

You have my hands cuffed so just twerk your waist and watch my mouth embrace while I taste everything you throw on me. I want your name on my face; I want it to leak down my bald head and everywhere. Yes I want the creamy crotch all over me. Now choke me a little. Yes put your hands around my neck and when you think I can't breathe. I will still have tricks up my sleeves. Now spin around and let's do this 69. Let me pump this dick down your throat, while you feed me your pussy praying that I choke. Let's try to cum at the same time. You should be in a hip hop video the way you are bouncing that creamy crotch in my mouth.

Keep bouncing, yes baby bounce harder. You scream and slurp, slurp and scream. I wish you will rise up and let me toss your salad. You cum down my throat and now your juice are pumping into my blood stream. You catch my juice in your mouth and we both scream. Then you uncuff me and begin to ride my dick. I grab the back of your ass for extra leverage. You are like a wild woman from the island, doing the dutty wine on this dick. Yes I love this shit. I am throwing this dick all in your ass until the bed comes crashing to the floor. I shoot a load off like a rocket and you release like a missile, together, we are weapons of mass destruction while we are fucking. I still need you to live up to your name, so while you are breathing hard and holding your chest. I'll roll you over and throw your legs to the ceiling. Yes baby I am your maintenance man, and I want to eat your cream until you scream. You are begging me to go deep so I go. What's my name? You scream Freknardo. I smile and continue to eat until you leave me with a creamy filled mustache above my lips.

I hear you talking Venus; I like the idea of you having a pussy that traps dicks and tongues. Just like the police, I am running up in your trap house and taking your shit. Planting these nuts in your ass and leaving seeds on your chest to digests. I'll handcuff your ass to the bed post, you the eighth woman I am leaving comatose. Since you like playing with fire, Consider this dick the roast, and I will roast your ass like a pig with an apple in its mouth. You like playing with balls all day anyway, so let me serve you mines. I like my pussy mean, sweet, and, smooth. You are a triple threat so let me suck your ass like I am angry, eat your ass like its candy, and suck your juices all night.

Your pussy might be good but I ain't falling in love with your ass. I'll tell you anything while I am all in that ass. I am one King that is willing to sit on the corner like a dog with a collar around my throat. I am a hungry dog, so lead me to your pussy and its murder she wrote. I am a nasty dog so I will pull your hair off your clit with my teeth, lick like a beast so feed me. No need to worry about my length because the way you will be screaming God, your neighbors will think you are trying to repent. I have enough feet on my third leg to dig deep into your Venus and suck the milk out of your way. I promised I will never be your next prey but I will be your judgment day. That means everything you value in life has comes to the end. When was the last time a man ate you while he did a back bend.

Yes I am on some space age shit. I am a damn alien from Mars traveling to invade your Earth. I come in peace but since you are Venus, your pussy is my enemy. I am ready for war, born for

battle, lived to see you squirt blood and cum. I am a mad dog, sick.
I will leave you dumb and mute. If you were a cat, I'll eat away
your nine lives. My bank is something you will never take. When I
return, you will want to work for me like I am a pimp and you will
be on the corner trying to sell your cake. I love pussy that taste like
gold, but I'll spit diamonds outta my mouth by the time I finish
eating your soul.

The doctors keep telling me that I was a normal woman a couple of years ago. They even said I was a nympho until I ran across a brother name Freknardo. They said he fuck me senseless, made me lose my mind and even crack a few bones in my spine. I scream every time I hear that nigga name. I even walk with a limp and I drool every time I try to speak. Ladies of Poetic Pussies, be careful when you fuck with that freak. Now I just look at the corner and stare at the walls. I will never be the same but Mama sometimes visits me and I'll always ask what happen to our family. Yesterday I receive a DVD in the mail and the doctors made me watch, praying that I could recall that night.

(FLASHBACK)

Yea Nut Nympho you like when I put your ass into a fucking pretzel. I am going to fuck your ass until one of your damn eye socket and veins pop out. Your sorry ass begging me to stop, asking a King to step down from his throne. You were talking all that shit before I invited you home. Fuck this, you going to be in a strait jacket by the time this dick is finish smacking. You shout Daddy I can't breathe, you going to break my neck. I keep slamming my dick in your ass because you don't deserve respect. Talking about how you can back shit up. You better not dry up. Now shut the fuck up. I am drilling that ass and the pussy is farting extra loud. I stop, pull out my dick, and made you kiss it.

27). Freaky as Fuck 10 out of 13

I fuck her ass until she had convulsion and shakes. I fuck her so hard that her head started to spin. I thought the pussy was possessed so I slaughter the demon, call me the high priest. She went from been freaky as fuck to barely walking. She was a good test subject, looking for multiple nuts. I heard she is freezing my sperm and drinking it every morning out of the cup. She told her shrink that my nut is her Vitamin C. My cum drops is the only thing that is keeping her sane. Poor woman, another Pussy down in this game. Who wants to fuck with the big bad Freknardo? I laugh every time I think how I came to her office, asking for some help. She had on these nice ass boots and tight skirt. I push her ass down and jack up her skirt, rip her panties off and went straight to work.

She was screaming security, I slap her ass and said nah it's just me. This time I wanted to show her more than just the dick. So I gave her the tongue tunnel, nasty to some but it left her ass in a coma. I twisted that tongue so deep in her ass hole and finger her pussy for fun. She was shaking and bouncing all over the office, begging me to stop. I had her ass cumming and pissing at the same time. Nasty but I love it and I kept fingering and licking until she gave up the ghost. She was trying to call 911 and ask for help. I said call your Mama as I slap her across the ass with my leather belt. I beat that ass and left whips all over that freak.

She loves it and kept saying Master please beat me. I fuck her until her eyes roll into the back of her head. I shook her to wake her but I thought the freak was dead so I fuck her like she was dead, Juicy

Corpse. I am laughing to myself as I tell this story. Now she is the one on TV and the news, telling the world my dick is the power and she is afraid to go to the bathroom to take a piss. The doctor is shaking his head as he write down everything on the list. She sometimes wakes up in cold sweat at night, praying that the dick don't come back to bite. I heard she wear a chastity belt around her pussy now. She is trying to protect herself from the freak that fucks from the moonlight to the morning sun. Last time I check the freak left her Pussy ass family and became a nun.

Yes Papi this is your pussy, Shut the fuck up, you fucking up my mood and then I hit you in the head with an eraser. I am not here to pleasure you but to take everything from you. I plan on eating your pussy and sucking out your eggs. I am a nasty freak and the more yawl talk, the more I take. See you been fending for this dick since I first came to your class. Yes you have been dressing like a poetic slut so I don't want your pussy, give me brain and butt. Yes you are going to be the first Puerto Rican tonight that I will fuck in the ass. I have your arms pent behind your back as I ram this rod so deep in your ass that you won't be able to shit for a week.

I was making love and making some of you all feel good. I guess you can blame it on that traitor that told me to pack this thick wood. Now I know you will need a sub to take your place as I cram this dick in your guts like a hard test. You like toys and shit. I know, be quiet while I am hitting it. I am fucking and jerking your body as you scream I been naughty Papi. I like dogging out my pussy and you are no exception. You just my freak, my damn freak. I own your ass. Once I get done fucking you in the ass, I am going to blow your mouth out, call it CPR, Cock, Pull, Release. I am such a fucking beast. Yes school teacher, I know all about you. I got an extra surprise for your filthy freaky ass. Passion Fruit get your nasty ass in here. She comes running with her strap on.

Hell yeah I am going to bed with a high on; we throw your ass over the table. She runs the strap on in your ass while you suck this hard dick. Passion can brag that she's not a traitor but she is my trick. She is fucking, and I must admit I like the way you are sucking. I guess being a school teacher has more brains than common sense. So I plan on making you choke as I grab your head and pull your face harder on my dick. Passion is tearing that pussy up from the back and loving it. She is screaming, I am fucking her good Daddy, I love working for you. I know Passion; keep fucking that Puerto Rican trick. You are being drilled out by a member of your own damn team. Then I take my dick out your mouth and bang it against your nose.

While passion is doing her best to make you suffer, let me help enlighten the mood. I reach in a bag and pour salsa on my dick. Then rammed it back in your mouth for fun, yeah suck it, you nasty school teacher. Don't worry baby, Papi will have some cream to mix with the salsa real soon. You are cumming all down the desk, Passion keep pumping and I took my dick out and jack my nut right in your face. Pull my damn pants up and watch the show.

Passion is a good Poetic Pussy that works for me. I pick up the phone and snap pictures of the Puerto Rican Butterfly been fuck by a member of her own team. This will be real good to post in Poetic Pimps. Nah I'll send it to the Queen of Poetic Pussy and tell her not only am I destroying your girls, I got them fucking for me.

29). Poetic Pleasure & Coochie Souffle 12 & 13 (Final Series)

I feel like Bruce Lee, the way I am kicking ass with these Poetic Pussies. I was on my way to destroy Coochie Souffle, then Pussy Pleasure roll out the closet. They were like Freak, this is the last nut you will skeet and we will restore power back to the ladies. I laugh because I knew after today; these freaks will be trying to recruit an army to fuck with me. I slowly strip out of my clothes and knew they were the Poetic Pussy last hope. I threw Coochie on the bed and let her suck the stroke. Pick Pleasure up and she starts to wrap her legs across my face. I ate her standing up, while Coochie blew my brains out. I was pumping her face hard, eating Pleasure even harder.

You should have seen the back of my ass bouncing these nuts in her mouth. My head had the same rhythm as I ate, and ate, and ate some more. I roll my tongue so quick in and out of her pussy until I tasted her cum. Then I nutted in Coochie mouth just for fun. I threw Pleasure on the bed and pick Coochie up. This time I sat on Pleasure face and fed her my dick while I let Coochie straddle my face as I ate her from behind. Yes I was eating Poetic Pussy raw and to the white meat. They were yelling and screaming we love you Freak. I love all 13 of yawl Freaks and I laugh as I continue on serving this dick. What's that smell? Nothing Daddy, you just the shit. I got these Freaks bodies shifting in all directions. So after Pleasure came, I sip and lick my fingers. She drops down and starts to eat Coochie. I begin to fuck her with some long ass strokes. Digging in her ass real deep like a miner, my dark sexy ass, nothing else is finer.

Now I am about to give them the force of nature as they both drops to their knees. I eat their pussy from behind to keep them wet. I started to fuck Pleasure doggystyle while I slap Coochie on the ass. They both were screaming Master Freak; we want this dick to lastttttttttttttt forever. I said why. They scream because no one else can do it better. I jump out of Pleasure ass and went right into Coochie, laying this dick down as the hardest foundation they have ever seen. They are howling like wolves at a full moon, begging me to stop abusing their pussy. I said shut up; I won't be done anytime soon. They love this dick and they are becoming addicts. I got all the Poetic Pussy pens ecstatic. They all want a piece of this dick, praying one lucky soul will turn me out. Every time I think about their weak ass, I drill these two freaks the fuck out. I am slapping Pleasure ass, while pulling Coochie hair. Cum bitch, cum for daddy, because they love that freaky shitt. I'm jump outta one pussy and into another one. You would think I am switching classes in college the way I am throwing this dick like knowledge.

Now I know the other 11 Poetic Pussies are on their way so let me finish off these freaks. I grab a vibrator and shoved it in Coochie ass, while I continue to fuck the shit out of Pleasure. I got them tricks yelling to the ceiling. I am thrusting, lusting, and giving them my stroke like the world is about to end. Poetic Pussy this is war, next time bring everyone you can think of. It took them forever to come together. I destroyed 13 freaks regardless of the weather. I did it on my own, I am thinking Freak you must be the King of the throne. Well I turn the vibrator up extra high and Coochie ass started to nut instantly. I told Pleasure to cum for Daddy and she did it without missing a beat. I said not a word to your family. Yawl just continue to eat each other out and respect that Freknardo is the King of Erotic Poetry. I pick up the phone and dial Juicy Dezire because she is nasty and I know she want to slob and spit on my dick. If only these Poetic Pussies knew that they were hanging with the enemy. Well I kiss the ass cheeks of Pleasure and Coochie. I know I am Poetic Pimps most wanted but yawl freaks will never take me alive.

30). Do Not Disturb

I just want to hold you, pull you close, and chain your soul next to mines. I want to chain you like a wild dog that ran away and it took me forever to find. See I been waiting for a minute to get all up in it. I told myself I was done with the erotic after last night, but you were complaining you wanted a poem of your own to set the mood right. See I'm about to chain you like a slave on the run, cut off your foot like Toby and keep the shotgun. I don't want you to go nowhere but to cloud nine. Watch as I chain my naked body next to yours, throw away the key, we ain't going to stop making love till we go half on a baby. See baby, this is black love to the highest power, no need to worry, we making love outside in the rain, so that's our shower. No need to worry about trying to eat, I'll swallow your heartbeat, and choke off the paint on your finger and feet. Baby is you feeling me. We are chain into a world where we are lock like super glue. If we were any closer I'll be swimming inside of you, making love so hard, my whole shadow will become you.

See Baby; just rub my bald head because I know Dreads are the thing these days. But consider I Samson and you can cut my hair and my power will still last for days. I will get lost in you like a maze; lose my focus and my speech. I want to stay chain to you till God take my breath away from me. See this is Do not Disturb, Tell the world to go away, Tell the World to take a day off, Tell the sun not to rise. If God created the world and said rest, then I want to create a universe with your black hole, find and search through your milky way, get lost in your rings of Saturn, circle around your Venus and dived into the deepest space till my mind become weak and erased. See you getting me in trouble been chained to you but you ask for a piece so I'm delivering everything I got in me. I'm keeping this clean because I don't want to be disturbed. The hurricane will not blow us down, The earthquake will not stop me from laying it down, and if it start lightning, then don't be frighten, I'm your thunder, I'll drink your ocean so don't worry about taking me under.

This is Songs of Solomon the 2010 edition. This is our chain of love, you can be my car and I'll be ready to start the ignition. We won't have time to argue because our tongues will be dancing to its own beat, too close to clap our hands and stomp our feet, So our ears will listen but our emotion will be on another mission. See I want to be chain to you everywhere, over there, down there, anywhere. Imagine us being chained in the middle of the freeway, making love as the traffic watch this foreplay, at a basketball game, right before the half time show. Just you and Freknardo. We can be chained together during the Talladega race, they would cancel the race just to watch us kiss and embrace. I think I'll stay chained to you for better or for worse, for sickness and health. Let's just make love till we are disturbed by death. Then we can make love in the afterlife, not be like the Egyptians, and marry me all over again in the next life. You can change your name but you will still be my wife. I'm chained to your soul, whipped by your command, do not disturb until God say that's enough man.